He lookeln't recognize; hich to compa nd she recognized his words immediately.

Jared was reciting a poem by Langston Hughes, a poem called "When Sue Wears Red," and he did it perfectly. He looked at her with all the reverence the great poet had intended, walking around her and taking in every detail of her essence; it was way beyond just her appearance, and she knew it. How he knew a poem by Langston Hughes she didn't know, but there was something else she knew for sure. When Jared finished the poem their fingers slid together and neither of them said anything for a moment until Alexis broke the silence.

"We're not going out, are we?"

Jared had pulled her into his arms and was holding her close when he answered. "Probably not."

She melted against him, her arms going around him trustingly as she tilted her head back to receive his kiss. "What do you want to do?"

He took his time answering because he was engrossed in the feel of her taut, sexy body against his own. "Everything."

Books by Melanie Schuster

Harlequin Kimani Romance

Working Man
Model Perfect Passion
Trust in Me
A Case for Romance
Picture Perfect Christmas
Chemistry of Desire
Poetry Man

MELANIE SCHUSTER

started reading when she was four and believes that's why she's a writer today. She was always fascinated with books and loved telling stories. From the time she was very small she wanted to be a writer. She fell in love with romances when she began reading the ones her mother would bring home. She would go to any store that sold paperbacks and load up! When she had a spare moment she was reading. Schuster loves romance because it's always so hopeful. Despite the harsh realities of life, romance always brings to mind the wonderful, exciting adventure of falling in love and meeting your soul mate. She believes in love and romance with all her heart, and she finds fulfillment in writing stories about compelling couples who find true, lasting love in the face of all the obstacles out there. She hopes all her readers find their true love. If they've already been lucky enough to find love, she hopes that they never forget what it felt like to fall in love.

Poetry
man

Melanie Schuster

HARLEQUIN®

entertain, enrich, inspire™

To all my faithful readers
who keep their love on top for me!
I love and appreciate you all.
And a special dedication to my brother Dwight Woods.
Thanks for being my rock and for giving me
the most beautiful nieces in the world.
Stay blessed!

Recycling programs
for this product may
not exist in your area.

ISBN-13: 978-0-373-86285-6

POETRY MAN

Copyright © 2012 by Melanie Schuster

For questions and comments about the quality of this book, please contact us at CustomerService@Harlequin.com.

www.Harlequin.com

Printed in U.S.A.

Dear Reader,

Thanks for coming along on another installment of Friends & Lovers. If you started with *Working Man,* then you know how the series got started with Nick Hunter and Dakota Phillips. It was followed by *Model Perfect Passion* (Billie Phillips and Jason Wainwright), *A Case for Romance* (Ayanna Walker and Johnny Phillips) and *Chemistry of Desire* (Emily Porter and Todd Wainwright). Now in *Poetry Man,* we have Emily's ride-or-die girlfriend Alexis Sharp's story of finding love with Jared VanBuren, finding true love in the most unlikely way.

Next March you'll find out all about Emily and Alexis's BFF, Dr. Sherri Stratton. As you saw in *Poetry Man,* Sherri has sworn off men until her precocious little girl, Sydney, is at least fifteen. But there are two people who have other ideas about the situation. One is Sydney, who's decided that her mommy needs a husband. And the other person is Lucas VanBuren, Jared's handsome younger brother, who agrees with Sydney that he'd make a perfect mate for Sherri. When these two put their heads and hearts together, Sherri won't stand a chance.

And yes, Alexis's sisters will find love in the near future because with these friends, love is never far away!

By the way, *The Nero Wolfe Cookbook* mentioned in my book is real; I'm a huge fan of the series by the esteemed Mr. Rex Stout and I use the cookbook regularly.

Stay blessed,

Melanie

melanieschuster@sbcglobal.net

I Chronicles 4:10

To all the DIVAS who have come before me and on whose shoulders I stand; all the magnificent and generous writers who have encouraged me along the way and made me believe that I could do it, too.

A special thanks to Evette Porter, Gwen Osborne, Sha-Shana Crichton and as always to Jamil, who still makes me laugh. And a very special thanks to Pam Beasley, who's my own ride-or-die BFF. Everybody should be blessed with a friend like Pam.

Prologue

Alexis Sharp took a deep breath before plunging into the empty pool at her health club. Alexis preferred to get her daily swim in early, before she went to work. She'd often wished she had a pool at one of her two beauty spas, but reality would kick in and she knew it was too expensive to install and not really what her customer base wanted. Her clients wanted top-notch hair care, facials, massages, mani-pedis and the like. What they didn't want was to get their expensive hair-dos wet. So, she made do with a daily swim that was as necessary to her as breathing.

The cool water stimulated her and gave her a chance to think. She was so busy running the spas, her volunteer work teaching water aerobics and being a swim instructor on the weekend that she often felt as if she was treading water when she was on dry land. She used her schedule as the reason why she didn't date; she was just too busy. However, she and her closest friends knew that wasn't the real reason she didn't make room for social interaction in her life. She'd had a normal dating life at one time. She'd been engaged, in fact; right up until the night she'd found her fiancé in bed with his ex-girlfriend. That had put a crimp in her feelings about men for quite a while. Plus the tales of romantic woe she'd heard from the women of her family since she was a small child. Her mother insisted that all the women of their family were doomed to never have a successful relationship with a man. If it was just her mother talking, Alexis could have overlooked it, but her grandmother, her aunts, cousins and her sisters all agreed that there was no point in any women in the family woman trying to fall in love because they had a love curse on them. It was all nonsense, of course, but when Alexis was adding up the reasons that men were off-limits in her current life, she'd think about her mother's pontificating with a grim smile.

Alexis swam vigorously for a while, enjoying the feeling of the water against her body. After doing about twenty laps, she turned over and floated on her back. She'd been swimming since she was about three years old and her enjoyment of it never flagged. Her love of the water was one of the reasons she kept her hair cut so short. And the fact that it suited her face so well. Glancing at the big clock on the wall, she decided she could stay in five more minutes. She had taken the day off because she was having her two BFFs over for lunch today and she wanted to make sure everything was ready. Not just the food, she wanted to get herself emotionally ready, too, because she knew that her friend Emily was going to interrogate her about her social life, rather her lack thereof.

After her dear friend Emily had surprised everyone by getting married out of the blue, Alexis had done an abrupt about-face and decided that she was going to find her own Mr. Right. She'd had enough of being alone and if Emily could find a tall, handsome doctor and start a new life, so could she.

After her firm declaration of her intention to meet her perfect mate, Emily was going to want to know about her progress and the fact was there wasn't any. It was both embarrassing and frustrating for a lot of reasons, not the least of which was that she was tired of being celibate.

There were times that her body drove her crazy with longing for a lover. Alexis had to admit there were times she wanted Mr. Right *Now;* she couldn't have cared less about Mr. Right. Alexis was a perfectly normal woman with perfectly normal desires. She couldn't sublimate her desires in her work forever; all the spa business in the world couldn't prevent her from wanting all the things that any woman wanted. Things like an understanding man, a good lover and plenty of really good sex. If she didn't get some soon her sheets might burst into flames from all the hot dreams she'd been having.

She stopped her lazy floating and turned over and started stroking again, swimming ten more laps before getting out of the pool. She was still alone because most people didn't start coming into the gym until later in the morning. Especially on a morning like this one, with pouring rain and the occasional clap of thunder. Thunderstorms were typical in Columbia, South Carolina, especially in the summer, but they didn't bother her at all. Alexis had always been fond of rain; she was a true water baby. She was patting off her face with her towel as she walked to the women's locker rooms. She'd almost reached the door when a really loud crackling arose, followed by a clap of thunder that sounded like an explosion. The room went black and Alexis had to stifle a scream as she collided with a wet man who was coming out of the adjacent men's locker rooms.

He was very tall, as her nose reached the middle of his chest. His arms went around her and hers went around him in an automatic response. His skin was damp from the shower all members had to take before getting in the pool, but he didn't feel clammy. Instead, he felt wonderfully warm and he smelled terrific.

"Are you okay?"

Alexis had to clear her throat before answering, because his deep voice did something to her, something really nice.

"I'm fine," she said. "Thanks for asking."

The lights flickered and it looked as if they were coming back on. Alexis seized the moment to back out of the tempting arms of the stranger and scoot into the locker room. She fumbled the handle on the women's side just as the lights began working again. She toweled off most of the water and got dressed in record time without stopping for a shower. She was normally cool and in control, but the feel of the tall man's body on hers had lit a fire in her. She wouldn't have been able to recognize him if she met him on the street because she hadn't gotten a look at him, thanks to her running off like a scared rabbit. But the brief encounter reminded her of just why she'd decided to get back in the dating game. She couldn't ignore her needs, wants and desires anymore. Maybe it was time she got back in the dating game and play until she won. Just once. If she played it right, one time was all she'd need.

Chapter 1

"So exactly when are you going to start dating, Alexis? I thought you had a big change of heart when I got married." Emily Wainwright, recently wed and soon to be a mother, accompanied her words with a sweet, teasing smile that Alexis would tolerate only from an old friend. Emily had been Alexis's bestie since elementary school, along with their other BFF, Sherri Stratton. The three of them were sitting around the table in Alexis's cute kitchen. Like the rest of the house, it was beautifully decorated; Alexis had really good taste. They were enjoying the lunch that Alexis had prepared when Emily had brought up what was once a sensitive subject. Sherri braced herself for a dose of Alexis's wrath, but it didn't come. Instead, Alexis laughed.

"I admit that I've been known to sidestep the dating scene, but I've actually been trying to do a little more socializing," she admitted. "And it's not the easiest thing in the world. Girl, dating is *hard*," she said emphatically. "Have some more salad?"

Emily was easily distracted by Alexis's offer of more crab salad and homemade rolls. Alexis heaped another helping of the delicious salad onto Emily's plate, while Sherri gave her another roll and refilled her lemonade. They loved spoiling Emily anytime, but especially now during her pregnancy. Since she'd eloped over Thanksgiving weekend and then moved to Chicago, they didn't have too many chances to dote on their girl.

"I'm probably eating too much, but this tastes so wonderful," Emily said happily.

"You can have anything you want, now that you're eating for two," Sherri assured her. Sherri was a doctor and spoke with authority on the subject. "You should gain about thirty-five pounds before delivery and you're nowhere near that yet. You've been taking very good care of yourself."

"I'm eating well and I'm still exercising and Todd keeps a close eye on me, whether I want him to or not." Emily sighed. Her new husband was a doctor, too, and his only desire in life was to keep her safe and happy. "And I'm actually eating for three," Emily said with a smile. "We just found out that we're having twins!"

After the exclamations of joy and excitement, Emily went right back to her initial topic of discussion. She was a biochemist by profession and nothing could deter her once she had marked out a path of inquiry on any subject. "Alexis, you vowed on New Year's Day that you were going to have a love life this year. You wanted the spare keys to the house on Hilton Head because you were going to meet the man of your dreams, kidnap him and spend next New Year's Eve having a passion-filled tryst. It's June. Halfway there. So what happened to those plans, Lex?"

Alexis curled her dainty upper lip in a gesture that was more snarl than smile. "Is it nice to rub people's noses in their

fantasies? No, it's not. It's very mean, as a matter of fact."
She rose gracefully from her chair and went to the refrigerator to refill the glass pitcher of lemonade. She always made the old-fashioned kind from scratch with fresh lemons and spring water. Hopefully being a good hostess would make her friend drop the subject. But her maneuver didn't work.

Emily patted the corners of her mouth with her linen napkin and held out her glass for more when Alexis came back to the table. "It didn't sound like a fantasy to me, Lex. It sounded like a declaration, a statement of intent. Your primary goal was to meet a suitable mate and develop a relationship."

Alexis didn't have a chance to refute Emily's remark before Sherri chimed in. "Not just a relationship, a marriage. I was there and I heard every word. And trust me, she's not doing anything that could possibly plant her feet on a trip down the aisle."

She and Emily laughed heartily, but Alexis didn't join in. She uncrossed her arms, which had been locked across her chest like an extra-tight sports bra. "It's not that funny, you two. I've dated enough lately to realize that the single pool is shrinking and stagnant and the likelihood of finding a mate is small. Infinitesimal, actually. So I've decided that I'm not looking anymore. I'm going to let him search for me," she said with a touch of defiance.

Sherri looked surprised and Emily looked thoughtful after Alexis made her announcement. She finished off her roll and took a sip of lemonade before speaking, but what she said let Alexis know that she was on her side.

"I actually think that's a good idea, Lexie. When you go out looking for something you almost never find it. I wasn't looking when I got together with Todd. He just kinda dropped into my lap. If the things you've been doing haven't been working, it's time to sit back and see what happens," she said. "What exactly have you been doing, by the way?"

Alexis gave her a grim smile that was less from humor than frustration. "I've been going out on some really bad dates. Really, really bad," she emphasized.

Emily's eyes widened. "Bad dates? How many and how bad? And what's for dessert? Wait a minute, don't tell me yet. I have to pee again." She pushed away her chair from the table and hurried to the bathroom.

Alexis had to smile as she watched her scurry off. It was hard to believe that less than a year ago Emily was a grouchy, rumpled academic with no interest in men whatsoever. After a surprise encounter with Todd Wainwright at her family's vacation home on Hilton Head Island, she and Todd fell head over heels in love. Now Emily was a newlywed with two babies on the way. She looked like a new person with her fabulous haircut, courtesy of Alexis, and a new wardrobe Sherri helped her pick out. Her beautiful caramel skin glowed with happiness and her demeanor was now anything but glum. She was cheerful and more outgoing than she'd ever been before. And it was all because she'd met and married her soul mate. Love could work miracles, if Emily was an example.

"What's for dessert? And what's up with the bad dates?" Emily was back, seeking truth and sweets.

"I have some homemade lemon bars if you refrain from asking questions." Alexis was an excellent cook and her lemon bars were better than any in the whole world. Emily was clearly torn for a moment, but she decided to play the mommy-to-be card.

"Sherri says I can have anything I want. And since your godsons or goddaughters are incubating inside me as we speak, I can't be denied," she said smugly. "So you can't make me choose between dessert and dish. Give it up or I'll whine," she warned.

"Oh, sit down. I'll tell you whatever you want, just don't make that horrible sound. You know I can't stand that," Alexis said grumpily.

"Good. I want two," Emily said, holding up as many fingers. When the pair of extra-big bars was set before her on beautiful pale green pottery, she grinned and took a huge bite. "So good! Now these bad dates— How bad could they have been?"

This time, Sherri and Alexis locked gazes and burst out laughing. When they could talk again, Sherri wiped her eyes with her napkin.

"They weren't just bad, they were atrocious," Sherri said. "If I hadn't been an eyewitness to a couple of these so-called dates I would swear she'd been exaggerating, but I was there and I saw it all. It's just ridiculous what passes for dating these days."

"Sherri saw them? Were they double dates or something?" Emily's face was alight with open curiosity.

Alexis sighed loudly. "These would have to fall into the 'or something' category. Sherri was my wingman a few times. She'd go with me and sit at another table in case things went south and they often did. Like with that jackleg preacher," she said with a shudder.

"How did you meet him and what went wrong?"

"Are you sure you've got time to listen to this drivel? Because if I try to tell you about each one it could take all day," Alexis warned.

"I've got plenty of time. Todd is with Mama, helping her to organize the rest of the things she wants to move to Chicago. Closing a house you've lived in as long as she lived there is more than a notion. He won't mind if we take our time. He adores Momma and the feeling is quite mutual. They just love each other. So if you can find me something to put my chubby pregnant-lady feet on, I'm good to go. After I pee again," she said thoughtfully. "I think they take turns jumping on my bladder. They must be boys because sweet little girls wouldn't do that to their mommy."

Sherri looked wise and shook her head gently as Emily went to the bathroom once again. "Sydney got in a few good kicks from time to time," she said, referring to her little girl. "She liked music and she'd dance whenever she felt like it. She also seemed to respond to football games because she loved marching bands. If a game was on, she'd be marching along in my belly like a drum major. As you know, I was sure she was gonna be a total tomboy but she's turning out to be a regular little princess. She still loves football, but only from the stands. Soccer and dance are her main interests for now. And yep, she used to tap dance on my bladder with great frequency."

"You don't have to remind me," Alexis said. "We were with you every step of the way, if you recall."

Emily came back into the kitchen in time to agree with Alexis's last statement. "Let's elevate my mother-to-be cankles, please. And then I want the real deal, no more stalling!" Emily said firmly.

"Fine, but don't say I didn't warn you, chick. These are some scary tales straight from the crypt of broken dreams. Don't blame me if you have bad dreams tonight."

After they retired to the comfortable living room and Emily's feet were propped on an ottoman, it was story time.

"I guess I should do this in chronological order," Alexis said thoughtfully. "That way you can see how my lovely hopes and dreams got smashed into bits on the ugly cliffs of reality."

Emily had to swallow a laugh. "You're still the queen of melodrama, aren't you?"

Sherri assured her that she was. "Some things never change."

"And you know this," Alexis said with a spot-on imitation of a royal wave. "Now, if you harpies would quit picking on me I'll tell Emily the sad tales of romance gone wrong. Sherri is my witness. I wasn't going anywhere alone with a strange man so I would have the guy meet me and Sherri would be there, too, discreetly, of course. Anyway, the first guy was a cousin of a very nice lady from my church. You know they always say that, when you want to meet someone, you should let your friends know so they can hook you up. And what's better than a church hookup, right? I was pretty sure that Mrs. Grice wouldn't introduce me to a serial killer, you know?

"His name is Herbert and he's a teacher. He's also getting a degree in theology, or so he said. Not good-looking, not bad looking, just average. No real personality, but he was pleasant enough until he told me I was the darkest woman he'd ever dated. And how surprised he was at how pretty I am."

Emily's eyes got huge and her mouth fell open. "Girl, no he didn't!"

"Oh, yes, he did. It was bad enough that he brought up the subject in the first place, but the dummy wouldn't let it go. He kept talking about it like I was the eighth wonder of the world or something."

Alexis was indeed the proud possessor of a complexion as dark as chocolate and as smooth as the finest silk. She was also extremely fashionable. She wore her glossy black hair in a short, chic style like Halle Berry's and it showed off her features beautifully. Alexis wore sleek, contemporary clothes in dazzling colors that brought out her rich coloring and made her look like the best-dressed woman in any room she entered. To some, Sherri, Emily and Alexis made an odd-looking trio. Emily was tall and brown, Sherri even taller and very fair skinned and Alexis the shortest of the trio with her chocolate-brown complexion. She had a hard time getting her head around the concept of being color-struck but there were still folks who clung to the idea that lighter skin was more desirable. It was so silly to Alexis that she generally just ignored the idea and all it implied. When she did stumble over someone who voiced their preference in pigmentation, it was like meeting someone who thought the earth was flat or who believed in alchemy. Alexis rarely encountered the outdated concept unless she was talking to someone who was really dense like Herbert.

Alexis could remember the exact moment when she knew Herbert was going to say something ignorant that would get him placed in her little red book of losers from which there was no hope of return. They met at the restaurant, which was his pick. It wasn't a four-star gourmet establishment, but it was nice enough for a first date, especially if the male wasn't foolish enough to expect after-dinner sex. That wasn't gonna be happening tonight or any other night, ever, no matter how needy she was. Alexis was her usual calm, reserved self, if she had to say so herself; she was ladylike and accepting of his humor; she contributed to the conversation in a friendly manner as long as it didn't veer into the ridiculous. When she caught him staring at her as if she possessed the secret location of the Holy Grail, she knew he was about to blurt out something she'd regret hearing and sure enough, he did.

"All the women I've ever dated have been either light skinned or very pale brown," he said.

Alexis wisely held her tongue because if she opened her mouth, she'd let go with a stream of vitriol that would land her on the local news at the very least, and quite possibly on the internet. Everybody had a cell phone these days; people who couldn't balance a checkbook knew how to upload scandalous videos to the web. Instead of lashing out at him, she adopted the expression she used when dealing with social misfits like Herbert. It was a bland, patient expression that gave away nothing but covered a variety of unpleasant reactions. To Alexis's delight, a large piece of lettuce had lodged itself between his front teeth and she wasn't about to tell him. It was much too pleasurable to observe his stupid grin with the random bit of greenery adorning it. He just kept rattling on, unaware of the fury that was mounting across the table.

"I've never dated anyone who couldn't go to a paper bag party," he confided. "But you're so pretty, they'd have to let you in even though you're so dark. Your hair even looks good, but it would be better long. How come you don't get a weave?"

Emily's laugh was choked off by a gasp of horror. "Girl, no he didn't! What an idiot."

"That was the main reason, of course, but he also took my doggie bag," Alexis said dryly.

"He did what?" Emily stopped in the middle of wiping away tears of laughter to stare at Alexis.

"We went to that Chinese restaurant that serves those huge portions. There was enough food on my plate for three people at least. I couldn't eat it all and I asked for a to-go box. He promptly confiscated it and took it home with him!"

Emily looked totally stymied by this revelation. "Well, maybe he…"

"Don't try to make excuses for him. He actually said something about how he paid for it and he should be the one to eat it. Sherri heard him because we were walking out to the parking lot and she was right behind us.

Sherri nodded her head vigorously. "Yes, he did, girl. He grabbed that thing like he had imminent domain or something. Latched on like there was a winning Powerball ticket in it and hurried to his car as if somebody was going to take it from him. But not before he tried to get a little sugar from the lovely Alexis." Sherri tried not to laugh when she said it, but a few giggles crept out, anyway.

Emily made a face. "He tried to kiss you? Ewwww!"

Sherri couldn't contain her laughter anymore. "He tried and succeeded, didn't he?"

"He mumbled something about 'gettin' a little sugar from his sugar' and before I could react his mouth was on me like a vacuum cleaner hose. I'm sure the memory of that impromptu embrace is going to haunt me for the rest of my days," Alexis said glumly. She brightened up and added, "But he's gonna remember it, too, because I kneed him right in his party favors. His *little* favors."

Sherri was howling with mirth and Emily had joined her, but Alexis didn't care at that point. It was a funny story, although it wasn't a testimonial for dating in a modern world. After a few minutes, Alexis reminded Emily that she had more tales to share.

"Well, when the friends-and-family intro program didn't bear fruit, we tried speed dating," she reported.

Emily gave a Sherri a surprised look. "Sherri, you went speed dating?"

"No, no, no! You know I'm not going to date until Sydney is at least fifteen. I don't have the time or the inclination to try and incorporate a man into our lives right now," Sherri said firmly. Sydney had just turned six and Sherri was determined not to complicate her child's life with an entourage of strange men. Alexis often told her that a few dates were hardly a parade but Sherri wouldn't change her mind.

"Sherri didn't participate in the speed dating. She just dragged me there and loitered around until I had to bolt,"

Alexis said. "And before you ask, yes, I absolutely had to get the hell out of there." She shuddered theatrically as she thought about the night in question. The event was held on a Wednesday evening at a popular restaurant/nightclub. The tables were arranged so the aspiring daters could face each other. In Alexis's mind it was sort of like what purgatory would resemble.

A couple of the men she talked to seemed nice, but they didn't strike any chords with her. One man she recognized as the husband of one of her clients. He had no idea who she was, but she definitely knew him. There was no way in the world Alexis could face sitting across from him, so she kept a keen eye on his progress. The bell rang to signal it was time to change partners.

"So I'm barely over the fact that a married man had the gall to show up at a public affair for single people when another guy sat down. He was tall, dark and handsome, believe it or not, and he was in PR or something. We actually had a decent conversation for about a minute until he said that he hoped I wasn't a democrat. That's when I noticed the little enamel Tea Party button on his lapel and I got up and walked out. I just couldn't deal with it," she said wearily. "Besides, if I'd stayed in my chair, my next 'prospect' would've been the married man."

Sherri and Emily knew how seriously Alexis took politics and infidelity so they didn't suggest that she had overreacted. Emily did have a question for her. "Have you ever thought about online dating?"

Alexis made a face. "Yes, I tried that, too. The results were less than stellar. I keep getting emails from boys who were too young and men who were too old. Lots of white men, for some reason. Why they found their way to a site called Mahogany Singles I don't know, but I was their pick of the week."

"Don't be so close-minded," Emily chided her. "Are you telling me you wouldn't date a man from another race?"

"Not if he's old enough to be my grandpa," Alexis replied. "I don't care about race. I just don't want to date senior citizens. If somebody bought me a Mercedes and it was blue instead of red, I certainly wouldn't hand back the keys," she said. "If a man has the right qualifications, who cares what color his wrapper is? I'm just not into antiques, that's all."

Sherri tried not to laugh but failed. "That is so wrong, Alexis! An older man might have a lot to offer. Wisdom, maturity, sophistication…"

"Age spots, wrinkles and a lifetime supply of Viagra," Alexis cut in sarcastically. "If you're interested, I have several you can email. One of them looks like he played backup for ZZ Top, except his beard is longer."

They were all laughing when Todd Wainwright came to collect his beautiful bride. Todd seemed to be perfect for Emily in every possible way. He was tall, gorgeous, brainy and he adored her. He cherished her so much that it would have been sickening had it been anyone but Emily on the receiving end of all that love. Alexis felt as if her friend deserved every wonderful thing that had come into her life and she was really happy for the two of them. They chatted for a while, until Todd announced that Emily needed to relax before dinner.

"You ladies will have to come up to see us soon," he said. "No more flying for her before the babies get here."

Once upon a time Emily would have had a sarcastic remark to rebut a statement like that, but all she did was smile and agree. "We're actually cutting it close," she said. "This is the beginning of my last trimester. I'm due in August but with twins you never know."

Alexis and Sherri walked the couple out to their car and

waved them off. Sherri gave Alexis a one-armed hug and re-minded her that she had to pick up Sydney from a play date. She got into her car and buckled her seat belt, but before she drove off, she had to drop some knowledge on Alexis.

"I just figured something out today, Lexie. The reason you're meeting the wrong men is because you don't know what you want in the right man. You need to make a list of every single quality you desire and then you'll know him when he finds you," she said.

Alexis frowned. "A grocery list for a man? That doesn't sound very romantic. It sounds kind of desperate, actually."

"Not really. What happens when you go to the store with-out a list? You come home with everything except what you went to get. You have to know all the characteristics you're looking for in a man before you throw yourself into the mat-ing pool. And I figured something else out today, too. You really don't want to date, you want to get married. You're looking for a husband, not a playmate. I could see it in your eyes when you were looking at Emily and Todd."

"No, I don't," Alexis sputtered.

"Yes, you do, and there's no reason why you shouldn't want to get married. You'd make a wonderful wife and mother. But in order to get that, you need to be very specific about the man you want to see first thing every morning. When you make that list, don't hold back. Include everything you can think of and then put one secret thing at the very bottom of the list. It has to be something that will truly touch your heart that no one else could ever guess. When you see that trait in a man, that's how you're gonna know he's your mate," Sherri said confidently.

"If you know so much about it, why aren't you hooked up? It seems to me that you're the one who should be on her way to married bliss, not me." Alexis was very fond of having the last word, but so was Sherri.

"Yes, but remember there's one big difference between you and me, chick. I don't want to get married. Go inside and start working on your list, I'll call you later."

Before Alexis could marshal up a reply, Sherri was backing down the driveway, waving merrily. All Alexis could do was stare at her friend with her hands on her hips and a little pout on her lips. She walked back into the house and poured the last of the lemonade over ice, deep in thought as she did so. She wasn't completely sold on the idea of making a list, but she did go into her bedroom, taking out a pretty navy blue leather journal she'd bought a couple weeks ago. Armed with her glass and her notebook and a pen, she went to her deck and reclined on a chaise, sipping and thinking.

Chapter 2

Despite Sherri's insistence that a list would make things easier in the dating department, it only made things worse. Alexis dutifully wrote down all the characteristics she was looking for in a man. However comprehensive the list was, it wasn't magic; even months later, the list didn't cause Mr. Right to show up at her door. She was sticking to her resolution not to look anymore, but she hadn't noticed a sudden influx of new men in her life. She told Emily so while they spoke via Skype that night. Emily was breast-feeding one of her sons and Alexis felt a pang in her own breasts as she watched. She was so fascinated that Emily had to call her name a couple times to reengage her in conversation.

"You aren't listening to me, are you?"

"Not really," Alexis admitted. "Where is Daniel?"

"I'm impressed. Most people can't tell Randall from Daniel. Daniel has already dined and his loving daddy is changing him and putting him to bed. So tell me what happened with the dating thing? We talked about this back in June and here it is, almost Halloween and you've done basically nothing to improve your dating situation."

"I told you I'm not on the hunt anymore. He's going to find me and so far he's taking his own sweet time."

Emily was about to say something when Todd came into view to scoop up Randall. He was bare chested and wearing scrub pants and the look of love he gave Emily made Alexis's heart turn over. After he greeted Alexis with a quick hello, he bent to kiss his wife and cradled their son on his shoulder, patting his little back to insure a good burp. Emily stared after him with the same besotted look in her eyes and Alexis suggested that they talk later, but Emily wanted more dating details.

"Emmie, there are no more details. I just haven't had any social intercourse to speak of, really."

"Wow. You made this decision way before the babies were born and now it's the end of October. But I really do think it's better to take your time than to mouse around with a slew of losers. Don't worry. Your man is on his way, trust me."

"He'd better get here soon because frankly I'm losing interest in the whole idea. I'm looking for a couple new spa locations, one in Hilton Head and one in Georgia. I've decided to be a tycoon. I don't have to look for anyone or wait for anyone to do what I do best."

Emily sighed deeply and ran her fingers through her hair. "Don't give up on love, Alexis. There's someone out there for you, I know there is."

Todd returned to the bedroom and soft music started playing. He had a tray with two flutes of what looked like champagne and a plate with fruit and cheese. This time Alexis insisted that she had to leave and Todd gave her a grateful smile.

"I'm not giving up, Emmie. I'm just not looking anymore.

If my Mr. Right is out there, he'll find me. Now it looks like *your* Mr. Right has some plans that don't include a third wheel so you go ahead with your evening and we'll visit again soon. Good night, you two." Before Emily could protest, Alexis got offline at once.

She stared at the computer screen and traced the outline of her lips several times, something she did when she was deep in thought. Without actually realizing what she was doing, she took out her navy journal and turned to the pages with her secret list. "Maybe I need to rethink this," she murmured as she picked up her pen.

Now that her list was complete, it occupied a permanent corner of her mind. Given the time of year, it seemed like an early letter to Santa Claus. She was headed to work in her cute little MINI Cooper Countryman. She loved the little car with its custom paint job; the roof was creamy ivory and the base was chocolate brown and it suited her perfectly. While she was fastening her seat belt, the list was still foremost in her mind and she started giggling at the Santa Claus idea. "Dear Santa, I've been a very good girl. Could you please bring me a burning-hot hunk of tall, dark-chocolate-colored love to have my way with on Christmas morning? I'll be a very bad girl then, I promise."

Alexis was still laughing out loud as she pulled into the parking lot of Sanctuary One, the first spa she'd opened five years before. When she crossed the employee entrance in the back of the spacious building, she was engulfed by the familiar scent of her home away from home. It was a combination of organic hair products, scented candles and the incense from the yoga studio. She inhaled deeply and smiled as she went to her small office to leave her purse and jacket. After she looked at her daily planner, she slipped on a fresh smock while she took off her taupe platform heels and put on her black wedges. They were just as high as her heels, but she'd learned the hard way not to wear light-colored shoes to work. One drop of tint was all it took to ruin an expensive pair of pumps. That was also why she protected her expensive clothes with a cover-up; one drip of peroxide or even permanent wave solution would wreck an outfit. This she knew from sad experience.

Alexis worked very few customers these days. Her emphasis was on managing the spas, not servicing customers. Hiring, training, managing the budget, advertising and other such areas were her bailiwick now. Besides hairstylists, she had aestheticians, yoga and Pilates instructors, nail technicians and manicurists to manage, in two locations, no less. But there were a few clients she continued to work on mainly because they were close friends and they simply wouldn't allow anyone else to touch their heads. She also liked to keep her hand in the various offerings so that her skills would remain sharp. Emily's mother was one of those ladies she couldn't abandon and, since she was in town, of course she was getting the full treatment today.

The salon was laid out in such a way that each patron had the luxury of some privacy due to the half walls that separated the stations, yet it wasn't so closed off that they couldn't chat with one another. There was something about being in a hair salon that encouraged even the most reserved women to relax. There was always pleasant conversation to go along with the soothing jazz that played all day, except for the early afternoon when the soaps were played on the wall-mounted flat-screen televisions. Alexis was making her customary preopening walk-through to make sure that everything was in proper order. It was always pristine and perfect, a tribute to her management and to the loyalty of her staff. All Alexis had to do was start the coffee and the water for tea, and she really didn't have to do that because her lead stylist, Javier, was already taking care of that.

He greeted her with a raised eyebrow and a grin. "One of these days you'll let someone else do things around here and we're all going to pass out from shock," he said dryly.

Alexis pretended to misunderstand him. "Oh, then I shouldn't have made those ultrarich brownies and pecan tassies last night? Well, shoot, I guess we don't need them here. I can just drop them off at church for choir rehearsal, I guess."

"Don't pay me any attention, I'm still half asleep," Javier said hastily. "Did you leave them in your office? I'll just go back there and get them and you can arrange them any way you like. Just ignore me altogether. You know I don't have good sense."

Nothing could have been further from the truth, of course. Javier DeLaCruz was very smart as well as being very talented. He was also quite easy on the eye with smooth golden skin, jet-black hair and eyes and a smile that brightened any room. Alexis sized him up as he left the room. He was a devoted and trusted employee of several years and there was no reason not to consider promoting him to a management position. He had the experience and education and the right attitude. Alexis would be foolish not to offer him a better position with a higher salary; if she didn't, he might leave and start his own salon. She was still mulling over that idea as she continued the opening procedure for the day.

One of the things that made Sanctuary so popular was the ultra-deluxe treatment of the clientele. Alexis always provided refreshments for her customers, hot coffee and tea along with fresh fruit and luscious baked goods that she often made herself. It was a practice that was as popular with the staff as with the customers, but there was no real need for her to make them herself. Alexis had a moment of clarity that told her she was doing too much. It probably came from the gentle little dig Javier made about her doing everything around the place. His remark had merit, and she was going to give it serious thought when she got home that evening. She knew she worked too hard and too long, but the results were well worth it.

Sanctuary One was all about relaxation and nurturing. It was decorated in soothing peach and green with lots of live plants and specially designed lighting. Sanctuary Two was similar in design, but it was robin's-egg blue and chocolate-brown. She enjoyed the brief moment of calm before the doors opened; it always gave her a sense of accomplishment as well as inner peace, but it didn't last long. The salon came to life first, as usual. Early morning appointments were very popular especially toward the weekend. Alexis had to bite her lower lip as she noticed that her receptionist was once again late. Plus, she hadn't called in to let anyone know she was going to be tardy, which was a requirement of all employees. Here was another thing to put on Alexis's must-do list: a serious talk with a backsliding employee.

As usual, Alexis didn't let her annoyance show, she merely took over the desk, checking in customers and fielding calls until her appointment arrived and the missing receptionist showed up. Luckily the two events occurred at the same time. Ava, looking pretty and flustered, hurried into her seat at the reception counter with excuses pouring out of her mouth. All Alexis said was, "We'll talk about it later."

She turned her full attention to Lucie Porter, Emily's mother. "Ms. Lucie, I have to say that Chicago agrees with you. As much as I miss seeing you when you're away, I can tell that you're really enjoying your new life in the Windy City."

Lucie was a lovely woman and she did indeed show every indication of having a rich, fulfilling life. "I'm having a ball, Alexis. It's wonderful being in the same city with my daughters and my grandchildren, but I'm also meeting some fabulous men," she confided.

Alexis wasn't really surprised to hear that. Lucie was pretty and vivacious and she attracted men in droves. She was a great dancer and Chicago was a dancing town. Sure enough, Lucie told her about a dance club she'd joined and how much fun it was. She also had new pictures of Emily and the twins, plus pictures of her other daughter, Ayanna, who had twin daughters and two teenage sons.

"They're growing so fast, aren't they? They're so handsome," Alexis praised. "Emily sounds so happy every time I talk to her."

"She is," Lucie confirmed. "Both of my girls are very happy with their husbands and their families. But truthfully, Alexis, I thought you'd be all married up and happy, too, by now. I expected you'd be married long before Emily," she admitted. "What are you waiting for?"

Alexis covered her surprise at Lucie's question by putting a terry wrap around her neck, followed by a pretty protective cape. "I think it's time for a touch-up on your relaxer and a trim. And you're overdue for some color, unless you've decided to leave it au naturel."

As she hoped, her words distracted the older woman. Lucie picked up a hand mirror and looked intently at her hair, particularly at the silvery strands that were beginning to surround her face. "Let's leave the color alone for right now. I've started liking the silver, believe it or not. I have a friend in Chicago who has the most beautiful white hair you ever saw. It's more like platinum, actually. By the way, she's going to be down here in a few weeks. Would you mind taking her as a client? I know how busy you are."

"Of course, Ms. Lucie, I'd be happy to. Any friend of yours is a welcome client of mine."

"Wonderful! I'll give her your card and let her know to

call you. Her name is Vanessa Lomax and she's a fascinating woman. I think you'll like her."

Lucie chatted happily while Alexis parted her hair, applied the protective base to her scalp and hairline and then carefully stroked on the cream relaxer to the new hair that had grown since then. After she smoothed the relaxer with the back of a wide-toothed comb and she could see that the hair was sufficiently relaxed, Alexis took Lucie to the shampoo area and made her comfortable before rinsing her hair thoroughly and washing it with neutralizing shampoo.

Lucie was perfectly content during the process. "Alexis, you have the most relaxing hands in the world. I have trouble staying awake when you start working on me," she confessed.

"I have magic fingers," Alexis said cheerfully. It was true, her customers always told her how sleepy they got as soon as her hands touched their heads. It was sometimes a problem when she was giving a haircut, especially to a man. It wasn't too bad with Lucie; Alexis was used to doing Lucie's long thick hair and the older woman's silence gave her time to mull over what she'd said about Alexis being married with children. She was so far away from that territory she didn't even know if she wanted to venture that direction. Maybe it was better if she stayed right where she was, doing what she knew best.

Her day ended long after it had begun, but Alexis was still wired up, and it wasn't from too much coffee. It was part exhaustion and part frustration that was making her edgy. After the spa closed its doors that night, she had to have a talk with her almost-always-tardy receptionist. They had gone into Alexis's office and Ava, the guilty party, started spouting off a long list of reasons why she was late. Unfortunately, she chose the one phrase that was guaranteed to drive Alexis batty.

"See, what had happened was…"

Alexis held up a hand and closed her eyes. Every time Ava started an explanation with "What had happened was," the end result was usually an argument.

"Ava, stop. Let's not go there, please. You have to get to work on time if you intend to keep this job. Any job, as a matter of fact. You can't expect your employer to fill in for you when you can't manage to get to work on time. You're way too casual about punctuality which is why you've lost so many jobs in the past."

A glimmer of panic went across Ava's pretty face. "You can't fire me. You told Mama you'd give me a job until I went back to school."

Alexis squeezed her eyes shut before opening them slowly. "Don't play the baby-sister card, Ava. It's only because you *are* my sister that I haven't bounced you out of here on your fanny. You have a lot going for yourself, kid. You're good-looking, you're smart and talented. Why you can't seem to pull yourself together and do something with all the gifts God gave you, I just don't know. But you need to stop playing the victim and start living up to your potential. Start with something small, like getting to work on time," she said pointedly, "then work your way up."

As usual, Ava didn't seem to absorb anything that Alexis was saying. Her next words were proof of that. "Can I move in with you? Mama is driving me crazy."

"You know, doing the same thing over and over and expecting a different result is the definition of insanity," Alexis said as she picked up her purse and set the alarm. "You keep asking me that question and the answer is always the same. No, you can't move in with me. And from what I hear, you're giving as good as you're getting in the crazy department. Mama isn't thrilled with you, either. I'll give you a ride home, but I'm not putting a roof over your head. Let's go."

"Can I have that purse?" Ava, having ignored all the advice her sister doled out, was on to the next thing, in this case, a fabulous Louis Vuitton bag she'd coveted for some time.

"Don't beg, it'll make people hate you," Alexis advised as she turned into the driveway of her mother's pretty brick home.

"I'm not begging, I just want to borrow it," Ava whined.

"You don't have to borrow it. You can have one just like it when you finish school and get a good job. Until then, Payless is having a BOGO. Tell Mama I'll call her after my book club."

"Book club, swim class, work, aerobics classes, my God, do you ever just sit your butt down and do nothing?" Ava got out of the car and slammed the door a little too hard for Alexis's taste.

"I'll have plenty of time for that when I'm dead. Slam my door again and you'll be walking home from now on, heifer."

The rain was pouring by the time Alexis left her book club meeting. She didn't mind, she was used to driving in the rain, even a downpour like this one. The meeting had been stimulating and enjoyable as always, even though the book wasn't her favorite genre. The books were funny and well written, but nothing Alexis could fantasize about. There was no way she could hook up with a vampire. It made her shudder to think about it. The idea of cold skin next to hers was daunting and the thought of somebody sucking blood out of her body was... A sudden thud made her snap back to reality. She stopped the car and checked all the dashboard lights to see if there was something internal going on with her vehicle. Finally she bowed to the inevitable and got out of the car with her little pink flashlight.

Damn, damn, damn. A flat friggin' tire! She hopped back in and reached for her cell phone. She hit the speed dial for AAA and waited to get through to a human. An eerily bright blaze of lightning preceded an unnaturally loud crash and her head almost hit her roof when a huge branch fell down in a shower of sparks, barely missing her hood. Crap. If it was like this all over Columbia, it could be quite a while before she got help. Alexis patted her chest in the vicinity where she imagined her heart was. She was normally quite calm, but the past few minutes had her really unnerved. That's why she screamed when she heard the tap at her window. Of course, when she saw a pale face with deep-set pale eyes and stringy wet hair she yelped again. "A vampire!"

The man looked puzzled and touched his ear to indicate that he couldn't hear her, thank God. She didn't need him thinking she was crazy; he looked nutty enough for both of them. She let the window down a bit so that she could talk to him, but she prudently locked the doors as she did so.

"Umm, yes, did you need something?"

He smiled a crooked, surprisingly sexy smile that did funny things to her while she tried to compose herself.

"I think you need something," he said. "I can see that you have a really flat tire and I can change it for you if you will open your hatch."

Okay, that wasn't what she was expecting. "Thanks, but AAA is on their way. I'm fine."

"Well, they're likely to be a while with the weather and all. I can get you up and running in about fifteen minutes," he offered.

Nice. The stranger outside her door was certainly a rock and the flat tire was definitely a hard place. This was how people ended up on those true-crime shows, accepting help from a stranger. He said he wanted to help her but he could probably gut her like a fish and string her entrails on the fallen branch in the road.

"No, really, I'm fine," she insisted. "Thanks for the offer, but I'm sure they'll be along in a few."

"Listen, I understand you not wanting to trust a man you've never met before. I have two sisters and you're doing exactly what I've told them to do. Tell you what. I'll just wait in my car until they get here so that no one bothers you, okay? I'm behind you and I'll stay there until your help arrives."

Alexis mumbled her thanks and put up the window while she tried to call her big sister. Alana was the owner and operator of Custom Classics, the best auto repair and remodeling shop in Columbia and if AAA couldn't make it, Alana could come get her in ten minutes. She hated bothering her sister, but sitting on a dark street with a wet weirdo behind her was just not a plan. Unfortunately, Alana didn't answer her phone. She tried her house, her cell and her office to no avail. Crap. She'd just have to wait it out. Her heart rate had completely slowed back to its normal rate and she was now calm enough to rummage around the car to find something sharp and potentially lethal just in case she had to defend herself.

The rain showed no signs of letting up and the thunder and lightning continued, accompanied by winds strong enough to blow down more branches around her. A particularly strong burst dropped another huge branch, along with a power line— complete with scary sparks that flew in all directions. Lovely. After that display, the stranger returned with a determined expression.

She cracked open the window again and before she could speak, he delivered a speech he'd apparently practiced.

"I know you don't know me well, but I promise you I only want to help you." He held out his cell phone to her as he continued to talk. "My name is Jared VanBuren and I have the police on the line so that they can hear everything that's going on. I explained the situation to them and they're willing to listen in so that, if anything goes wrong, they'll be here in like five minutes to arrest me and save you. Go ahead, talk to the dispatcher, he's waiting."

Alexis stared at the phone, and then directed her wide eyes to the tall, soaking-wet man who looked less like a vamp now. He looked more like a Samaritan. She took a deep breath and put the cell phone to her ear. This was turning into the strangest day she could ever remember and she knew without being told that she wouldn't forget it any time soon.

Chapter 3

Alexis was feeling slightly silly for her distrust, but only a little. She talked to the dispatcher and was fairly sure of two things when she finished. One was that the police knew where she was in case things got weird, and the other was that this Jared VanBuren wasn't going to do anything to her that would end up on the late news. She was actually feeling grateful to her Samaritan for his insistence on doing a good deed. It had been over ninety minutes since she'd called AAA and a tow truck had yet to materialize, but Jared, bless his heart, had attended to her tire with speed and skill. The rain hadn't let up and she'd tried to keep him from drowning by holding her snazzy leopard-print Christian Dior umbrella over him as he worked, but he'd refused.

"Look, I can't get any wetter than I already am, so you just sit in the car until I'm done. Better yet, get in my car so we don't have to worry about the jack falling or anything." He guided her to his Range Rover and helped her in, a nice touch considering the circumstances. Alexis had a real thing for a man with nice manners. She appreciated the dry interior of the luxury vehicle as she inspected the SUV. It was very clean and tidy, except for some papers in a folder on the dashboard. Nosy as she was, she was dying to look through them, but she restrained herself. She did wonder what *Seven-Seventeen* meant, though; she saw the words on the folder and tried to figure out what they signified.

Suddenly all her attention was focused on her car and the man fixing it. Jared let out a yell that scared her half to death and she scrambled from the Range Rover to see what had happened. She was greeted by Jared holding his arm, his very bloody arm.

"Heavenly Father, what happened?"

"The jack slipped when I was taking it off. It's nothing," Jared assured her.

Alexis took one look and disagreed vigorously. "That doesn't look like nothing to me, far from it. I'm taking you to the emergency room."

Ignoring his protests, she reached into the hatch and came up with a brand-new package of chocolate-brown towels intended for Sanctuary Two. Luckily she'd just gotten a shipment that afternoon. Quick as a cat she wrapped his forearm tightly a few inches above the cut and told him to keep his arm up. It was obvious they couldn't drive her car because it was blocked by the fallen tree limbs. She wasn't too sure about driving his gigantic Rover, but a police cruiser showed up just then and the problem was solved. Alexis didn't have to explain much after the officer saw Jared's condition and before he could insist it wasn't necessary, they were all on their way to the nearest emergency room.

Alexis didn't even blink at going into the E.R. with Jared. She hated hospitals, but he'd gotten injured on her behalf, so she felt as if she owed him. It wasn't crowded, thank good-

ness, and the blood that was flowing freely from Jared's arm
had him in an examining room in no time. The nurse who
got him situated informed Alexis that she could wait in the
lobby but Jared protested.

"Family only, sir. She'll be right out there in the waiting
room." The nurse was an attractive black woman in her for-
ties and she was polite but professional and firm.

"She's my fiancée," Jared said calmly. "She's the closest thing I've got to family and I'd feel much better if she
could stay."

The older woman, whose name tag read Honor Jackson,
didn't blink an eye. "In that case, she's welcome to stay. Why
don't you take that chair while I get Mr. VanBuren ready for
the doctor?"

After Mrs. Jackson situated Jared on the examining table
and set up a tray with the instruments needed to suture the
wound, she slipped out to fetch the doctor. Alexis had a
chance to really look at her "fiancé" and she had to admit
that he was a fine specimen of man. He was about six-five
with blond hair, high cheekbones, a deep cleft in his chin and
deep-set eyes that were a striking shade of blue. No, gray. Or
were they green? Whatever color they were, they were mesmerizing. And he had a body that wouldn't quit, she could
see that quite plainly since Mrs. Jackson had helped him
remove his shirt so it wouldn't get cut off when the doctor
started working on him. She was rather glad the shirt had
come off because he had a spectacular torso; long and lean
with smooth perfect muscles. Her eyes were so busy assess-
ing his biceps and his abs that when he spoke it startled her.

"Hope you didn't mind that fiancée thing. I just wanted
company," he admitted.

His voice was mellow and soothing like cognac on a cold
night. To her surprise she wasn't upset about his ruse. On the

contrary, it seemed kind of sweet. Besides, to her mind it was her fault he was injured.

"No, I don't mind. Of course, I'm going to hold you to it," she said with a mischievous smile. "I'm expecting a ring before Christmas."

His eyes widened with mirth and they laughed together. "As you wish. Big or huge?"

"The ring? Gigantic, in case I have to pawn it."

He had a good sense of humor because he laughed again. They were still laughing when the doctor came in to inspect the wound. His name was Dr. Patil and he was the real down-to-earth type as he proved with his first words.

"That's nasty. Looks like you nicked an artery in there," he said as though it was the most normal thing in the world. "Hope you don't do a lot of manual labor because you'll need to take it easy for a few days. You're going to have a lot of stitches."

Alexis felt her stomach turn over. She really hated hospitals, doctors' offices, blood, gore and anything close to it. And she'd feel really awful if he had to take sick leave from his job.

Jared just shrugged. "It's okay. I'm opening a couple restaurants and it'll be a few weeks before I have to actually do anything in the kitchen. I'll be fine."

Dr. Patil was busy cleaning the wound. "So you're a restaurateur. Is this your first one?"

Jared winced as the doctor gave him a shot to numb the area in preparation for the sutures. "I have six. When these are finished, I'll have eight, maybe nine because I'm thinking about putting one on Hilton Head."

He winced again as Dr. Patil put another shot in the same area. "This is the worst part," the doctor assured him. "In about ten minutes I'm going to stitch you up and you won't feel a thing. Your fiancée can hold your hand and it'll be over before you know it."

As if she didn't have any control over her movements, Alexis went to his bedside and took his free hand, holding it tightly as though she'd been doing it forever. Jared gave her a wicked wink and kissed the hand that clasped his.

"That's it, baby. I feel better already." His hand tightened on hers slightly and he looked at her intently. "God, you're pretty. You're absolutely beautiful, I hope you know that."

Normally Alexis would have jerked away her hand and left the room, but she went along with it and leaned over to kiss him on the cheek. "I'm going to get you back," she warned him in a whisper.

"I wouldn't expect anything less," he murmured with an even sexier smile.

In a few hours, Alexis found herself on the receiving end of an inquisition. She was finally at home, facing both her sister and Sherri. Her car was safely home, too, thanks to Alana. She'd listened to her voice mails and had come to the rescue. The fallen tree limbs had been moved so that the car could be driven away, so she arrived at the hospital in time to see Alexis emerging from the emergency room entrance with a tall, gorgeous blond man in a wheelchair. Alana's calm demeanor didn't slip a bit, even when the man was referred to as Alexis's fiancé. She merely raised an eyebrow when Alexis informed her that the man, Jared, was going to need a ride home because he'd been given a painkiller that made it impossible for him to drive.

Sherri had also showed up at that point and after a short discussion, it was decided that Sherri and Alexis would take Jared to his rented loft and that Alana would meet them afterward at Alexis's house. Alexis was all too keenly aware that Alana was killing herself not to laugh at the situation, especially after Jared grandly informed her that he was looking forward to having her as a sister-in-law. Sherri drove to

Jared's building and it took both her and Alexis to help him to the elevator and into the big, barely furnished loft. It would have been a clean escape for the two women had it not been for Jared's kamikaze-like move that resulted in Alexis getting a good-night kiss from him.

"You saved my life," he informed her with a goofy grin. "That means I belong to you now."

"Jared, tomorrow morning, when the medication wears off, you're going to have a totally different perspective on this." Alexis was trying to be pragmatic and logical, but he looked so sweet and charming that it was difficult.

"Nope. I know what I know and I know that you're mine." And before she could utter another word, he planted a big, delicious kiss on her surprised lips.

"Jared, you must lay down. Your prescriptions are right next to the bed and I put a big glass of water there for you. If you get dizzy or nauseous, call the E.R. or call me. I left my number there, too," Sherri said in her most professional doctor voice.

"I just need Alexis's number. We're getting married, you know."

"So I've heard," Sherri said cheerfully.

Alexis had reached her limit. She made her small hand into a gun and pointed the forefinger at her temple, silently mouthing the word *BOOM.* She took one of Jared's long arms and Sherri took the other and they walked him over to his bed.

"Go to sleep or the engagement is off. Call me in the morning and I'll come take you to your car. Where are your pajamas?" She looked around in vain for anything that resembled sleepwear.

"I sleep au naturel. Wanna see?"

"Sherri, what the hell did they give him? Is he ever going to recover or is he just crazy?"

Jared was finally lying across the bed and looked as if he

was about to nod off. Sherri was biting her lip to keep the laughter that was building up inside her to a minimum.

"He'll be fine. Some people just react very strongly to those kinds of meds. We'll leave the light on for him and you can check on him tomorrow. Now, let's get out of here and get you home. You got some serious splainin' to do, sister."

And that's how Alexis found herself seated across the table from her sister and her best friend, recreating the evening's events. They were deriving a great deal of enjoyment from her explanation and Alexis had to admit that it was pretty funny when she told them how it came to be.

"I left the book club and I was thinking about the book we'd discussed when I got a flat. The lightning and thunder didn't bother me, but that nasty slap-slap-slap noise a flat makes scared the crap out of me. I called AAA, then I tried to call Alana, but I couldn't get you. So I was ready to wait it out and I was wondering how a sane woman could get hooked up with a vampire and then Jared tapped at my window and I screamed 'Vampire!' because that's the first thing that popped in my head."

Alana couldn't hold it in anymore. She started laughing and it didn't look as if she was going to ever stop. All of the Sharp women looked somewhat alike; slender with perfect cocoa-colored complexions and beautiful teeth. Alana's hair was longer than Alexis's. It was shoulder length and she often wore it in a ponytail to keep auto paint, grease and other kinds of soil out of it. She not only owned Custom Creative, she worked there everyday. No one looked less like a mechanic than Alana, but no one was better at her craft.

"You called him a vampire? Oh, that's too much!"

"He looked like a vamp, thank you very much! He was all wet and his eyes were all funny looking and he's so pale he glowed in the dark! Yeah, I called him a vampire! We had just been discussing *Dead to the World* and it hit home, that's all."

Sherri had to get her two cents in at that point. "He didn't look wet and drippy when I met him. He looked a little rumpled, but that man is really handsome! He couldn't keep his eyes or his hands off you, Alexis. So are you going to date him or what?"

Alana laughed again and the sound was beginning to grate on Alexis's nerves. "They don't have to date, they're engaged, remember? He kept calling her his fiancée and told me he couldn't wait to be my brother-in-law," she said with an evil grin.

"I told you, he said that so I could stay in the examining room with him. He wasn't serious. It was just a little joke between us that got a little out of hand when that pain medicine kicked in. In any case, I'm going to call him in the morning and get him to his car, if necessary, and that's that."

Alexis left her seat and began taking off her nasty, bloody clothes right there in the kitchen. "I should send him the bill for dry cleaning this outfit, but he did change my tire so I'm going to let it slide. But no, we won't be going out. He's not my type."

Alana's phone went off and she answered it as she walked to the living room, leaving Sherri and Alexis alone. "How do you know he's not your type?"

"I just do, that's all. He's not attractive to me," she said firmly.

"You need to pull out the list and see how many of your desired characteristics match his personality. You might be surprised."

Alexis ignored her and went to her bathroom to get the robe that was hanging from the hook on the door. "Sherri, I love you and I love my sister but you are both dead wrong about this. Jared VanBuren seems to be a nice man, but he's not the one. Nope. Now, while you pick up Sydney from wherever you stashed her to come rescue me, I'm going to take a shower. And tell my big sister to go home and read *Car and Driver* or whatever she does at night. Thanks to both of you but I've had a hell of a day."

Sherri wasn't that easy to dismiss; she had to have the last word. "After you get out of the shower, make sure you take a look at your list before you decide Jared isn't the man for you. That's all I ask, just take a look."

"Yeah, right, whatever. I'll get right on it."

Chapter 4

The morning after his adventure with Alexis, Jared woke in a great mood. His forearm still ached after getting the stitches, but as injuries went, it wasn't too bad. He'd gotten many worse injuries in the restaurant business, other cuts and burns that required trips to the E.R., but none had resulted in meeting a woman like Alexis. He stretched lazily under the sheet that covered him and smiled. He was enjoying the feeling of his morning arousal as much as the memory of kissing her. She probably thought he was crazy, but that was okay. He'd exaggerated the effects of the painkiller slightly, but it was so he could get her guard down and make her feel at ease with him.

Alexis Sharp was gorgeous, funny and sexy, and he was going to get to know her better while he was in Columbia. He was going to be living here on and off for months, until his two newest restaurants were up and running and he saw no reason to go without companionship for the duration. The restaurant business could be grueling, especially if you were the executive chef and owner. He was lucky that he had good business partners. His brothers Lucas and Damon and his best friend, Roland, were excellent partners which is why their empire was growing so rapidly. They were aiming for steady, sustained growth as opposed to flooding the market with a bunch of quasi-gourmet-of-the-month franchise eateries. His dream was unfolding as he desired, but a lot of personal sacrifice was involved, as well occasional inconveniences.

He'd planned on opening a restaurant here months ago, but he couldn't find a property to his liking so he had to build from the ground up. He also couldn't locate the right equipment for the kitchen, so construction was currently held up while he waited for the delivery of the custom ovens and cooktops from England. It was a pain in the behind, but it gave him time to search out Hilton Head Island for a potential spot and better yet, it would also allow him time to get to know Alexis better. That chocolate-colored skin, those flashing eyes, her luscious lips… He groaned and stretched again. She was a great kisser. Kissing her could be a part-time job as far as he was concerned.

He smiled again when he heard "Soulful Strut" by Young-Holt Unlimited playing; it was the ring tone he'd chosen for his phone. The smile got bigger when he looked at the caller ID and saw it was Alexis calling. "Good morning. Did you sleep well?"

A slight pause let him know that he'd caught her off guard. "Actually, I did sleep well. And you?"

"I was drugged into oblivion, thanks. I owe you another thanks for dragging my lanky self home. Most people would have left me in the emergency room to fend for myself."

He could almost feel her smile over the phone. "I'm not most people, I'm special. Besides, I'm in your debt. You rescued me and got injured and I felt responsible. In fact, I should probably pay your hospital bill."

His eyebrows lifted in surprise. "Don't be silly. You owe me nothing. Besides, I have insurance. What I could use, however, is some assistance getting the Rover back home."

He was so enthralled with the sound of her voice that he barely listened to her reply. Her voice was velvety and rich like chocolate ganache. It had a low, sexy pitch and he wondered if she sang. She had to; just hearing her talk was like listening to a song. He was so caught up in his enjoyment of her sultry tone that he had to yank himself back into the moment when she repeated a question.

"Sure, yes, I can be ready. You really don't mind coming to pick me up?"

"Not at all. I'll be there in about thirty minutes, is that okay?"

"Perfect. See you soon."

Now he was totally energized. He got out of bed and went to the kitchen for plastic wrap to cover his bandaged arm so he could shower. His habit was to do as much as possible in the shower to save time and water, so he brushed his teeth, shaved and bathed, emerging from the huge stall clean and cheerful. He dressed quickly, in jeans, a chambray shirt that was so old it was more white than blue and a pair of Crocs. They weren't the most attractive shoes in the world, but for someone who was on his feet most of the day, they were lifesavers. He combed his blond hair and thought about getting a haircut. It was down to his shoulders and it didn't bother him, but it drove his mother nuts. Her current aim in life was to get him married and she was sure that his hair was sending out the wrong message. He could hear her words as clearly as if she was in the room with him. "Sweetheart, I think you need to cut that hair. You'd look much sexier and sophisticated with a really good cut. How are you going to meet the right woman looking like a scruffy line cook?"

His eyes crinkled in a smile. His mother never bit her

tongue when it came to expressing her opinion on anything, especially when it came to marrying off her oldest son. He ran his hand through the long, drying strands and shrugged. Since he wasn't trying to land a wife, he saw no reason to worry about the length or style of his hair.

Turning on his iPod, he glanced at the clock on the docking station and decided that he had enough time to make Alexis something delicious for breakfast. There was no point in being a Cordon Bleu–trained chef if he couldn't impress a beautiful woman with an impromptu repast. He set to work, getting out the ingredients for biscuits, sausage and omelets. The *mise en place* was critical to any good cook; having everything at one's fingertips made the process of meal preparation much easier.

A knock on the door surprised him. Surely that couldn't be Alexis already? He didn't know any prompt women other than his mother and his two sisters. He thought that timeliness was a genetic trait because he'd never witnessed it outside his family. He answered the door and there was Alexis, fresh and sweet-smelling like a spring flower. He was so taken with the sight of her that he almost forgot to say hello, but his innate good manners kicked in.

"Good morning, Alexis. You look absolutely beautiful."

She was wearing a short trench coat in a soft gray color and under it he could see something in a tangerine color that made her complexion glow. Her hair was sleek and glossy and she had three earrings in each ear, a tiny gold post and two small gold hoops. She smiled at him and remarked that he used the word *beautiful* a lot.

"Only when it's appropriate, as it is now." He held out his hand to her and led her into the large room that comprised the main living space of the loft. "Please come in and let me take your coat. Since you were nice enough to help me reclaim my car, I thought a little breakfast was in order."

Alexis looked as if she was about to refuse but the smell of the coffee coming from the kitchen area was too enticing. "That's right. You told Dr. Patil that you were opening a restaurant. You made breakfast for me?"

"I'm just getting started. Can you stay or do you need to go to work or something?"

"Actually, I took the morning off. And I love to eat, so you may be creating a monster here. All I ask is that you let me watch. I like to cook," she confided. "Any time I can pick up some techniques from a pro is a good time for me."

Jared helped her remove her coat and felt a tremor of arousal as he saw that the tangerine color was a soft, thin tunic sweater that wrapped around her slender frame like a lover's caress. Her slim-fitting black jeans made her butt look spectacular and he had a hard time taking his gaze away from her. After he hung up her coat, he took her hand again and walked her to the kitchen area. He was pleased to see her eyes light up as she observed his array of utensils and ingredients. She went to the sink and washed her hands thoroughly.

"*Mise en place* before anything else? That's the way I try to do it. Not just because I've read about it so often, but because if I don't, things get a little catastrophic," she admitted.

"Then you have good basic skills. That's one of the first things you learn in culinary school." Jared rummaged around in a small closet and emerged with a big white chef's apron which he proceeded to put on Alexis. It covered her entire front and almost came down to her ankles.

"I don't want anything to happen to that beautiful sweater. The color is fantastic on you, by the way."

Alexis laughed softly. "You could bottle that charm and make some serious cash," she teased him. "So what are you fixing today?"

"I'd planned on omelets with sausage, sweet potato hash, biscuits and peach preserves. How does that sound?"

"It sounds fabulous. What do we do first?"

"First we make the sausage. I normally make links but I haven't found a supplier for the casings I like, so I'm going to make little patties. I hope you like salmon."

Her eyes widened. "My absolute favorite. I've never had salmon sausage before."

"I like to make home-style food. I'm not too crazy about trendy food and weird ingredients. My aim is to make the best American-style food with the freshest ingredients possible. I make several different kinds of fish sausages, as well as chicken and turkey."

Alexis looked mesmerized as she carefully watched everything he was doing. His knife skills were amazing. Alexis was pretty good with a knife, but compared to Jared, she was a rank amateur. "Where did you study cooking?"

"After I graduated from Indiana University, I went to Le Cordon Bleu in Paris. I'd made a deal with my parents. If I finished my business degree and I still had a passion for cooking, they'd pay for me go to Cordon Bleu, since I was nice enough to get a full scholarship for undergrad. I've always known I wanted to be a chef, but Pop wanted to make sure I could do it right as far as the business side was concerned."

"What does your dad do?" Alexis asked curiously.

"Pop is chief of surgery at John Stroger Hospital in Chicago. My mom is an educator in sociology. You would think that they'd discourage a nonacademic pursuit, especially for the oldest son, but they're not like that. They always encouraged us to follow our passions and it's worked out for each of us. I have two sisters and two brothers and we're pretty diverse, but we're all happy. Do you want to make the patties while I start the hash?"

"Oh, absolutely! But I want to watch you make the hash, too. I've never had it before. You're very creative with ingredients, aren't you? When did you get the urge to cook?"

"Watching my mother and my grandmother. Pop wasn't much of a cook, but my mom could throw down in the kitchen. In everything, actually, she's an amazing woman. When her mother came to live with us, I saw where she got it from because my gran is like a magician in the kitchen. So that's where I got started."

They continued to talk and prepare the meal together and the time just flew. In less than an hour they were seated at the breakfast bar, dining on Jared's amazing menu of plump, fluffy omelets with shallots, red peppers, spinach and Parmigiana-Reggiano cheese with smoked salmon, a delicious hash of sweet potatoes, fingerling potatoes and more shallots with Granny Smith apples and a bit of cream. The salmon sausages were bright with flavor and his biscuits were so light they melted on the tongue. Jared loved watching Alexis eat. Her obvious enjoyment of everything was turning him on to an amazing extent. He was far too used to women who picked over their food or followed some strange diet that prevented them from partaking in a good meal without a running commentary on how many calories and carbs they were ingesting. Alexis certainly wasn't cut from that cloth.

"You know, all we've done is talk about me. Now we're going to talk about you," he said firmly. "What kind of work do you do?"

Alexis took a sip of her excellent coffee and sighed with repletion. "I should be a competitive eater because I do love good food. I own two spa salons here in Columbia, Sanctuary One and Two."

"And how did you decide to go into the beauty business?"

"I always loved playing in someone's hair. I have three sisters and I loved experimenting on them. My aunt suggested that I get my cosmetology license so that I could finance my college education, so I did. I took vocational courses in high school in addition to my regular course load and when

I graduated, I had my license. I landed a scholarship to college, but I also worked as a stylist while I got my business degree. Scholarships don't cover everything, as you probably know. Is there any more coffee?"

"For you, anything." Jared refilled her cup and offered her the cream.

She thanked him and continued her story. "It just seemed to be a natural fit for me. If a salon is run properly, it can be very lucrative and my little salon got bigger and bigger and I started offering more and more services and I finally found a much bigger building and Sanctuary One was born. Then the second one. I'm thinking about opening another on Hilton Head, but I'm proceeding very carefully because of the economy."

Jared was fascinated by the account of her career. They had so much in common it was uncanny. It was as if he'd known her for years, not the relatively few hours they'd actually been acquainted. But he was going to change that and soon.

Alexis glanced at the clock on the kitchen wall and rose gracefully to start clearing the table.

"What are you doing, beauty?"

"I'm clearing the table so I can help clean up the kitchen. We've got to get your car before it ends up being towed or ticketed or something."

"No lady ever clears or cleans up in my house, darlin'. I appreciate your offer but it's not gonna happen here. Sit down and I'll have everything taken care of in about fifteen minutes," he assured her.

"You're too sweet, Jared. How have you managed to stay single?"

"A question my mother asks regularly, I assure you. I haven't given marriage too much thought, to be honest. But of course, that's all changed now."

Alexis gave him a quizzical look, which made him smile. "Have you forgotten that we're engaged?"

About an hour later, Alexis was following Jared to the site of his restaurant. After making the remark that they were still engaged, he'd laughed and she'd laughed along with him. It was still pretty funny. Just a silly joke between new friends, that's all it was. But there was a little bit more to it for Alexis, some nuances that she was trying to ignore. Jared was the first man who'd ever made her go weak in the knees from a kiss. She had tossed and turned all night thinking about the way he kissed and feeling every kind of dangerous sensation. And when she wasn't tossing around rumpling the bedclothes, she was thinking harsh thoughts about Sherri and her powers of persuasion. The stupid list continued to raise its annoying little head. Sherri had talked her into creating it, then insisted that she haul it out to see how closely Jared matched the list of "must-haves" that she'd committed to paper. She'd done it all right, and the results were rather unsettling.

Her list wasn't complicated, but it was specific. She could recite all twenty-five items on it from memory by now. She was looking for a man who was:

1. Tall
2. Dark
3. Handsome
4. Kind
5. Open-minded
6. Intelligent
7. Good manners
8. Honest
9. Family-oriented
10. Dog lover
11. Politically aware
12. Ambitious

13. Compassionate
14. Good sense of humor
15. Wants children
16. Generous
17. Likes to dance
18. Creative
19. Outgoing
20. Well-groomed
21. Affectionate
22. Passionate
23. Financially secure
24. Good kisser
25. ???

The last item was the secret, the one thing that only she knew and that she wouldn't tell; he would have to reveal it in order for her to know that he was really the one for her. Oddly enough, Jared seemed to have quite a few of those characteristics. He was tall, for sure. Dark wasn't going to happen with him, but he had enough handsome to share with several others. He certainly had a good sense of humor and he was an astounding kisser. And today he'd revealed several facets of his personality which were right there on the list: more good manners, his creativity, ambition and intelligence. Plus, she had discerned other things about him that she liked, things she hadn't put on the list. All in all, Jared VanBuren was quite a man. He was the kind of man she could spend a lot of time with and enjoy every minute of it. So he was vanilla instead of dark chocolate or anything close to it. Was that really the deal breaker, in this day and age?

Jared's Ranger slowed down and she had to jerk herself back to full attention to avoid a collision. He pulled into a parking space in front of a big building and she followed his lead. Before she could open her door, he was there, holding her door and offering his hand for assistance.

"Here we are at Seven-Seventeen, the site of my newest restaurant. Would you like the grand tour?"

Alexis didn't hesitate. "Yes, I would. It looks huge, Jared."

He unlocked the door and ushered her inside. "It's big, but it's not all dining space. There's a separate entrance and work area for a culinary school," he explained. "We started this in Chicago and the model worked so well that we're expanding it. It's a work-study program that we began in cooperation with the local high schools. It's a way of involving kids in a potential career path by getting them some hands-on experience and instruction."

Alexis looked up into his gorgeous face. "So the program helps the restaurant, too. You get free labor while the kids get low-cost classes," she said thoughtfully.

Jared shook his head and put his arm around Alexis's shoulder. "They don't cook in the restaurant kitchen. It's too fast, too dangerous and too much potential for disaster. I'm trying to give them a viable learning experience—I'm not trying to exploit them for free labor.

"The students get school credit, they get work experience and they get paid. Plus, the whole community benefits because anyone who wants to dine at the restaurant can do so and pay whatever they can. There's too much hunger in this country and too much food goes to waste, so this is my way of narrowing the gap."

Alexis was happy that his arm was around her because her knees started doing the accordion fold again. She could check a few more boxes off the list from what he'd just told her. His arm tightened as she leaned against him for support. Things could get really complicated if she wasn't careful. She looked up at Jared and his ocean-colored eyes were warm and, if she wasn't mistaken, affectionate. Before she could panic, he lowered his head and kissed her again. Whatever she was thinking drifted away completely and she lost herself in the feel of his mouth on hers.

Chapter 5

Now it was time to give Alexis a tour. After Jared led her all around the restaurant, pointing out every unique detail of the layout and design, he'd been reluctant to leave her. Since there was no work taking place at the site today, he had a free afternoon and he wanted to spend it with Alexis. He liked everything about her. She smelled better than any other woman he'd ever been with. A sweet, provocative fragrance drifted around her that teased his senses and drove him into a mild frenzy of desire. Her perfume was as intoxicating as her personality and the way she kissed was probably illegal in several states. He couldn't seem to stop touching her, which was unusual for him; Jared wasn't normally the touchy-feely sort. But there was something about Alexis that made him extremely reluctant to let her go.

When they'd seen every nook and cranny of the facility, he stopped walking and stood in front of her holding both her hands and smiling down at her pretty face.

"Are you hungry? We can go to lunch," he told her. "I've been checking out the competition around town and it would be a big help if you came with."

Alexis looked intrigued, but her words weren't the ones he wanted to hear. "It's a little early for lunch, at least for me. Besides, I have to go to Sanctuary," she reminded him.

It took him a moment to remember what Sanctuary was; for a split second he thought she was referring to some kind of political asylum. He had a wry grin as he told her of his mental slip and was gratified when she burst into laughter. Her laugh was as warm and sexy as everything else about her and he planned to keep her in stitches as often as possible.

"Since you're not going to a safe house," he said drolly, "I'll go with you. After all, I showed you mine so now you have to show me yours."

She laughed again and her soft fingers gently squeezed his. "Cute. But it's liable to be boring," she warned him. "I have a client, too."

Jared raised her hands to his lips and placed a lingering kiss on each one. "I couldn't possibly be bored with you, Alexis. And I'd really like to see your spa. I know it's got to be as spectacular as you are."

"Well, since you put it like that, how can I say no?"

When they arrived at Sanctuary One, the place was busy as always. Jared was fascinated; it was simple and elegant like Alexis, and the combination of services she offered was more than one would have expected in a city the size of Columbia. Not that Columbia was a hamlet by any means, but there was a style about the place that would have fit perfectly in New York, Chicago or any other urban giant.

"You did this all by yourself? And you have two of them? You are an amazing woman, Alexis. Just amazing. This is a world-class operation," he told her.

"Thank you, Jared, that's nice to hear."

"I'm really impressed with the fact that you're so busy during a recession. Has it affected your business much?"

Alexis nodded emphatically as they walked to her office. "I saw the potential loss of business as a challenge," she told him. "It's taken a lot of creative marketing to keep the clients coming in. I, well, that is, my staff and I, had to come up with ways to create more traffic." They had reached her office and she invited him to sit on the comfortable love seat.

"That's the best way to approach it," Jared agreed. "I hate that phrase 'thinking outside the box' because it's become so clichéd, but that's what you have to do."

"I had a sales contest and tasked my staff to come up with marketing plans. The best ones would be implemented in the salon as well as winning a weekend at Hilton Head for the person who came up with the idea. They really rose to the challenge, too. We've partnered with a bridal salon to offer special wedding packages for the brides and their wedding parties. We do prom specials that include fashion consultations photography. Also, we have a salon squad that goes to nursing homes and senior apartment complexes to style hair and offer yoga and Pilates."

Jared's eyebrows rose. "You're brilliant," he said. "That's why your business is thriving when so many are struggling."

"It's not just me," she said emphatically. "My staff is just the best in the world. And they understand about keeping their eyes on the prize, too. We lowered the prices on some services and let the clients know that we did it because we understand that everyone has money concerns right now. We also started some reward programs, like discounts for referrals, special rates for group treatments like birthdays, bridal showers, anniversaries and what have you. It's a lot of hard work and a whole bunch of team effort, but we've been thriving, thanks to my wonderful employees."

Before Jared could reply, one of her darling employees came charging right into the office without knocking or otherwise announcing herself; it was Ava. She wore a look of innocence as she handed a note to Alexis, but Alexis knew she was just being nosy.

"Mrs. Fox had to cancel because her daughter went into labor," Ava said sweetly.

"Have the phones stopped working? Are the computers down?" Alexis's voice was as sweet as Ava's, but Ava recognized the tiny veiled threat in her words. What Alexis was saying was that Ava could have sent her a text, an email or picked up the phone to deliver the message; Ava was just trying to find out who the tall handsome man was. And Ava's gaze was all over Jared, who'd risen from his chair when she entered. She was lapping him up from head to toe. Alexis issued a tiny sigh and introduced her.

"Jared, this bit of mischief is Ava Sharp. Ava, this is Jared VanBuren. She's my baby sister as well as the receptionist here and I'm sure that she has something to do that pertains to answering phones, greeting customers and staying out of my business," she said.

Ava didn't heed the warning in her sister's voice, however. She stayed right where she was, smirking and simpering. "You look so familiar, Jared. Where have I seen you before?"

"You haven't seen *Mr. VanBuren* anywhere, Ava. Goodbye."

Ava's brow was wrinkled in thought and she continued to stare at Jared, who looked amused by the scenario. Ava's eyes widened and she gasped. "I saw you on the Food Network! On that show where you have to cook things to win money!"

Jared grinned and admitted he'd been on *Chopped*. "You have a good eye. Yeah, I was a judge a couple times."

"Have you ever been a contestant?" Ava asked eagerly.

"Ava, I think you're needed up front," Alexis reminded her.

"No, I'm not."

Alexis tilted her head slightly. "Is that so? If that's the case, you can leave. I guess I don't need a receptionist, after all," she said pointedly.

Ava had the good sense to rethink her last statement. "I meant to say, I've got to go, I'm needed up front," she said quickly as she disappeared through the office door.

Jared laughed as Alexis shook her head with a soft little sigh. "You can pick your friends but I had no choice whatsoever with Miss Ava."

"She's adorable. I can tell she's a handful, but she's cute. So I've met your older sister, Alana, and your younger sister, Ava. Isn't there another one in the mix? Didn't you say you had three sisters?"

"You have a good memory. I have one more. Alana is the oldest, I'm the second oldest and Ava is the baby. Between me and Ava comes Adrienne. She's nothing like any of us, actually. We all kind of look alike, but she's quite iconic in every other way," she said dryly.

"I can't wait to meet her, and your mother, too."

At Alexis's look of surprise he gave her a wicked grin and reminded her that it was customary to meet the bride's family before the wedding. Alexis moaned and covered her face with her hands. Peeking at him between her fingers, she told him to cut it out.

"This may be a top-notch spa but it's a beauty shop at heart and you don't even want to think something that you don't want to be repeated. If this ends up on the Net tomorrow, I'm putting all the blame on you."

"Go ahead, I can take it. I do have a question for you. Since your appointment canceled, how would you feel about me as a substitute? I think it's time for a haircut."

"Not a problem," she answered. "I can do that, as long as you keep the engagement remarks to yourself."

"On one condition. We go to dinner tonight someplace really nice," Jared countered.

Alexis smiled as she rose to walk to leave the office with him. "I think that can be arranged."

Jared was quite comfortable and relaxed in Alexis's styling chair. He looked around at the private area she used for her clients and appreciated the simplicity and good taste of the design. It was spotlessly clean and there was absolutely no clutter anywhere, yet it wasn't sterile. It was a perfect reflection of Alexis's personality and he was about to tell her so when he felt her hands on him and he lost the ability to speak. She'd put on a neat, professional smock to cover her tangerine sweater, she'd laid out her combs and scissors on her counter and she'd put a cape on him to protect his shirt, so it wasn't as if he didn't know what came next. But he hadn't imagined the sheer electricity her fingers unleashed as she gently massaged his scalp. It was like a lightning storm had started in his groin and radiated through his entire body.

"I'll give you exactly five hours to stop that."

Alexis laughed and kept her fingers moving. "You wish."

"I do. That feels incredible. You have magic hands or something."

"And you have dry hair. There's a little discoloration on the ends, too. Do you swim a lot?"

"Just about every day of my life since I was a kid," he admitted.

Alexis stopped examining his hair. "Do you swim here?"

"Yeah, at a gym with the largest indoor pool in the area. I try to go every day."

He could see their reflection in the mirror and was surprised to see her expression change from calm to confused.

"I swim there, too," she said softly.

Jared raised an eyebrow. "You swim in the morning, don't you?"

"Yes, I do."

"And you were there the morning the lights went out, weren't you?"

"Yes, I was," she said, her voice lowered to a mere whisper.

"So you're the mystery woman who's been keeping me awake night after night. We bumped into each other and before I could find out who you were and ask you to dinner and a movie and propose marriage to you, you disappeared," he said with great amusement. "You felt so good in my arms and you vanished before I could even get your name."

He turned the chair so they were facing each other and put his hands on her hips to pull her closer. "You know what this means, right?"

"It doesn't mean anything, Jared. It was just one of those things, just a coincidence," she protested.

"I don't believe in coincidences. I believe in fate and this is ours. What are the chances that I'd have a semi-erotic moment in the dark with a sexy wet woman I'd never met and a few weeks later, I'd not only meet her on a dark and stormy night, but that we'd be engaged?" His tone was playful but his eyes were totally serious. He pulled her into his lap so fast that all she could do was grab his shoulders and hold on for dear life.

"Jared, you seemed so sane," she said sadly. "You're crazy, aren't you?"

"I'm totally and completely sane, beauty. Quit wiggling around and sit still, I'm already way too aroused under this cape thing."

"Can you just let me up for a minute? I have a Taser in my purse and I may have to use it on you," she warned him.

Jared's arms tightened around her. "How about we forget

the haircut and we just go to dinner or something. We have a lot to talk about."

"No." She looked flustered and sounded breathless but determined.

"Oh, yes," he countered.

"Absolutely not."

Jared kissed her chin and smiled. "Let's compromise."

Chapter 6

Alexis couldn't quite believe that she was actually going out with Jared, but she was. His idea of a compromise seemed harmless and it actually made sense in a way, so she agreed to it. Her cheeks got hot when she remembered his exact words, but that didn't stop her from replaying the conversation over and over as she showered and changed for their date.

"Listen, beauty, I know this seems crazy and I'm sure you think I'm certifiable, but something exceptional is happening here and we have to explore it. Fully. If we don't, I'm going to regret it for the rest of my life and die with your name on my lips."

She remembered how he looked into her eyes so intently that she felt it, a ripple of sensation spreading through her body. His eyes deepened to the color of the ocean and she felt as if she was floating away until she snapped out of it and wiggled off his lap. She backed away from him and pointed her index finger in his face, about to let fly with some really profound profanities but he'd gently grasped her hand and captured her fingertip with his lips. She thought seriously about passing out from the sensation, but he repeated his suggestion that they work out a compromise.

So he'd managed to keep his remarkably nimble hands to himself long enough for her to give him a superlative haircut and it was decided that they would go to their respective abodes until he came to collect her at eight for dinner. It was almost time for him to arrive, although Alexis had little faith in the ability of a man to show up on time. She had showered and shampooed and while her hair air-dried, she used copious amounts of body butter, followed by lotion in the same scent. After that she applied makeup, finished her hair with a blow dryer and a curling iron, all while her mind was racing like a cat chasing a laser pen.

Why am I doing this? Why didn't I just take him to his car and run? Why is he so freaking handsome, and sweet and funny? What am I supposed to wear? Where did he learn to kiss like that? Who knew he was my mystery man in the gym? How many more checks am I gonna put on that damned list? What am I going to wear?

When in doubt, wear red. The great Bill Blass originated the phrase, but it was a mantra of her mother and a motto of her mother's sister BeBe, who were her main fashion icons. Besides, she looked fabulous in red and tonight she needed the heavy armor of impeccable grooming for protection. Alexis loved color and the bright, rich shades she favored worked wonderfully with her chocolate-colored skin. She decided on a jersey wrap dress with long sleeves that she always pushed up to show off her deceptively delicate forearms. The silk-and-cashmere-blend fabric draped itself around her as if it was made to order just for her. Gold hoops, gold bangle bracelets and her four-inch black pumps completed her ensemble.

Okay, she was ready. She was dabbing a little more eau de parfum between her breasts when the doorbell rang.

The digital clock read 7:55 p.m., which made her smile. Another check mark for Jared; he was prompt. She was still smiling brightly when she opened the door to find Jared on the porch with a big bottle of wine and a bouquet of deep red roses.

"Wow." They said it at the same time, just like a scene in a romantic comedy.

"Come in, Jared. Those are just beautiful," she said, indicating the flowers. He nodded without saying anything, which struck her as odd.

"Well, let me get a vase and then we can leave." She led him to the living room so that she could get the vase that adorned one end of the mantel. Jared still hadn't said a word, although he followed her. Before she could reach for the vase, Jared carefully placed the bottle of wine on the mantel and laid the flowers next to it. Then he held out his hand to Alexis, who very delicately placed her hand in his, as though she wasn't sure she wanted it to stay there. He looked at her in a way she didn't recognize; she had nothing with which to compare it. Finally he spoke, and she recognized his words immediately.

Jared was reciting a poem by Langston Hughes, a poem called "When Sue Wears Red," and he did it perfectly. He looked at her with all the reverence the great poet had intended, walking around her and taking in every detail of her essence; it was way beyond just her appearance, and she knew it. How he knew a poem by Langston Hughes she didn't know, but there was something else she knew for sure. When Jared finished the poem, their fingers slid together and neither of them said anything for a moment until Alexis broke the silence.

"We're not going out, are we?"

Jared had pulled her into his arms and was holding her close when he answered. "Probably not."

She melted against him, her arms going around him trustingly as she tilted her head back to receive his kiss. "What do you want to do?"

He took his time answering because he was engrossed in the feel of her taut, sexy body against his own. "Everything."

In less than a minute they were in her bedroom. It was perfectly neat and looked pretty and feminine, but the décor wasn't Jared's primary concern at the moment. All he was thinking about was the sexiest, most beautiful woman he'd ever been with in his life. Jared walked backward to the bed and sat down, holding both of Alexis's hands. They were small and soft and he could feel her pulse beating as her wrist rested on his palm. A light was on the table next to the bed and it was just perfect, not too bright, but enough so that he could see every bit of her. He pulled her to him so that she was standing between his long legs. He'd dressed up for their first date and it seemed as though he was wearing an awful lot of clothes. He needed to get them off, but he didn't want to stop touching Alexis. His hands had made their way to her hips, and he was stroking them up and down, enjoying the feel of the soft fabric and her firm body.

"Pretty dress. You look gorgeous, by the way."

Alexis surprised him by stepping closer to him, pushing his suit coat off his shoulders and kissing him at the same time. "Thank you," she whispered. "You clean up very well, did I mention that?"

Jared didn't answer, he was too busy touching and stroking her. "How does this dress fasten?"

"I'll show you if you get rid of this jacket and that shirt."

Jared stood up and had the offending garments off before she finished her sentence, kicking away his shoes and unfastening his pants before he sat down again. "Show me. I want to undress you."

Alexis giggled, a low sultry sound that made him even more aroused. He followed her instructions and untied the dress, opening it to reveal the treasure he was seeking. Her bra was red, too, trimmed in black lace. She had on a matching thong panty and garter belt which was attached to silk hose and the total image was one he'd never forget. As her dress fluttered to the floor, he ran his big hands up and down her arms, then her waist, and then he palmed her butt, squeezing it gently as he memorized every inch of her.

"I thought you were in a hurry," Alexis said in a throaty, teasing voice.

Jared stood up again, this time removing the rest of his clothing so that his chiseled body was completely naked and his massive erection showed his mood quite plainly. He picked up Alexis and placed her in the middle of the bed before kneeling over her. "I'm trying to make this last forever, beauty. We only have one first time. But if you want more, well…"

He found the front clasp of her bra and undid it before bending down to taste her breasts for the first time. He loved her small, perfect breasts with the big dark nipples. He licked one and closed his lips to suck gently until it hardened and bloomed like a ripe berry. He turned his head to give the other one the same devotion and was gratified to feel her tremble underneath him. She breathed his name and he captured her mouth in his, gently sucking her lips before devouring her lips and tongue. He continued to explore her mouth as he massaged her swollen breasts, enjoying the sounds she was making. Finally he relented, kissing and sucking down her neck and chest as he worked the tiny thong off her pretty behind and down her thighs. The pumps were long gone, but

he wanted the stockings on so he left the garter belt alone
for the time being.

Alexis was quivering under his touch. His long fingers
began to explore her womanhood and he watched her intently as he stroked between her legs. She was already wet
and wanting him, he knew by the fragrant juices that were
already flowing. Using his middle finger, he rubbed her cli-
toris, stroking it gently but firmly, waiting until he knew she
was about to reach a climax. Suddenly his finger entered
her body, moving inside her, searching and stroking until he
found what he was looking for. Her hips were moving and
her face was flushed with passion when he changed positions so that his mouth joined his hand. His mouth closed
over her jewel and he used his tongue to drive her further
into the frenzy he'd started. His finger deep inside her, he
sucked harder and harder until he felt her climax. Her tight
muscles squeezed his finger and he felt the hot flow that sig-
naled her release. She was moaning and sighing and he didn't
want it to stop. He kept drinking her sweetness and using his
hand to give her more pleasure. He could feel her hands in
his hair and the pumping of her hips and it brought him to a
higher level of arousal. His tongue and his finger were moving in the same rhythm, wringing everything from her until
she cried out loud and shook from the force of her orgasm. It
continued on and on and Jared went with it, slowly removing
his fingers so he could cup her butt with both his hands and
bury his face between her thighs. Her long legs were over
his shoulders and she ground her hips against him as his hot
mouth coaxed even more sensations from her.

Slowly, very slowly, they began to come apart; Jared continued to pleasure her with his tongue as she sighed with
repletion and they changed positions so that she was on top
of him, trembling all over and slick with sweat. Her nipples
looked foreign to her eyes; they were huge and hard and they

felt so tender that she couldn't wait for him to start tasting them again. He was about to wipe his face with the back of his hand when she stopped him. She kissed him wildly, rubbing her cheek against his, licking his face and kissing him again, sucking his tongue for long moments as she moved her hips against his hot, sweaty body.

"Jared, baby, what was that?" She sounded dazed and happy.

He laughed gently and finished stroking her back before rubbing his hands in circles on her butt. "That, baby, was your G-spot."

"I read somewhere that science doesn't believe it exists."

Jared laughed. "So who do you trust? Your own body or some nameless, faceless science geek? What do you think?"

Alexis moved so that she was straddling Jared, rubbing her wet womanhood on him. They were sitting up, his arms around her while she stroked his broad chest with her small hands. "I think you're a magician," she murmured.

"No, baby, we're magic," he corrected her. "The two of us make magic together." He was playing with her nipples, his thumbs rubbing them softly as he smiled at her. "Come closer," he invited, and when she did, he put his mouth on one of the hard drops of dark chocolate and began to suck on it gently.

Alexis trembled all over and her body began to move again. "Harder, Jared, do that harder," she whispered. He obliged with more pressure as his hand massaged the other side. Her eyes closed and she suddenly needed to be even closer to him. Her legs spread wider and she reached down to take his hard, heavy manhood in her hand. She was going to stroke it and caress it but she found herself guiding it into her body because she couldn't wait any longer. It was so big she didn't think it was going to make it in as she tried to guide it to her target. He took over and rubbed the tender, fully engorged tip back and forth, letting it bathe in her wet warmth. Alexis moaned softly and her breathing became labored and erratic until Jared pushed hard and they were locked together. She wrapped her arms around his shoulders and his hands went around her waist as they moved together to form the perfect pace. She almost screamed from the sheer sensation of being filled to the brim but Jared began thrusting upward and she had no choice but to follow his lead.

It felt so good that she began to climax almost at once. He was so big and thick that every thrust rubbed her jewel and sent waves of pure pleasure all over her body. Jared could feel her heat, he could feel the sweet juices flowing all over him and it made him harder and hotter. He thought he could go all night until Alexis's walls tightened on him and squeezed. She pumped and squeezed until he knew the inevitable was coming. They were holding each other tightly when the earth-shaking climax came for both of them, a sensation that rocked him to his core. Eventually they collapsed, sweaty and shaking from the shared passion. Jared was the first to recover. He kissed Alexis's face all over, ending with a long, lingering one on her temple.

"I'll be right back," he said as he got out of the big bed. Alexis admired his long body as he went into the bathroom. He looked as good from the back as he did from the front, especially his butt. And he was obviously not self-conscious in the least, something that she found rather endearing. She got up, too, frowning a little as she looked at her love-rumpled, expensive silk duvet. The label said dry-cleanable; she hoped it was accurate. She fluffed it up and folded it down to the foot of the bed before turning back the sheet and blankets. While Jared was occupied, she decided to take advantage of the other bathroom and tended to a few things, including brushing her teeth and finger-combing her hair. She planned on being back in bed before Jared discovered her missing, but he surprised her. She slipped into the bedroom to find him waiting in the bed. Two glasses of wine were on the bedside table, along with the roses which were now in a vase. He gave her a dazzling smile.

"You're not shy, are you?"

Alexis smiled back at him, loving the way he was enjoying her nudity. "Not a bit." She continued walking toward him but his words stopped her.

"Whoa, wait a minute, beauty. I want to get a good look at all of you."

"Like this?" She obligingly turned like a runway model so that he could see everything, including the provocative heart-shaped patch that was the result of her meticulous pubic waxing. Her dark skin gleamed in the light of the candles Jared had lit and the evidence of his enjoyment showed in the erection that was clearly visible under the sheet.

"You're a goddess. Come here, and let me worship you," he said in a playful growl. She was next to him in two seconds, wrapped in his arms and laughing with pleasure. His mouth covered hers and she opened her lips to him. The taste and feel of his kiss was familiar and delicious, just like the feel of his hands all over her body. The sweet sensation was building again and she was ready for more when he suddenly stopped.

"Alexis, wait, stop, wait. I didn't use a condom last time and that was just wrong and careless on my part."

She was touched by the sincerity in his voice, but she still indulged in some mischief. "Suppose we just made a baby?"

His eyes crinkled in a big grin. "It'll be beautiful, that's for sure. Can you imagine what a pretty baby we'd have?"

Bemused, Alexis started rubbing his hard stomach in circles. "We don't have to worry about that tonight, I'm on the pill. And I'm perfectly healthy. I've been without male companionship for some time and I had myself tested before and after my last liaison."

Jared kissed her forehead and said, "I've also been tested and I'm cleaner than the board of health, plus I never go bareback, at least until tonight. You just felt so good, I forgot myself and my years of prudent behavior. But I have to tell you something—I don't know why someone as divinely sexy as you would choose celibacy but I'm thrilled you changed your mind."

Alexis continued to explore the flat planes of his six-pack as he spoke. He was smooth and shaven, something she hadn't expected, but it was sexy as hell. She took him in hand and began to touch him and taste him, causing an immediate reaction.

"I'm supposed to be worshipping you," he said in a slow, sexy voice.

"If I'm the goddess, you have to do what I say, right? Then I command you to lie back and enjoy this," she said in a throaty whisper. There was no more talking as she applied a long, lingering kiss to the broad head of his manhood. Her tongue went around and over the smooth skin and her hands slid up and down the thick pole, cupping the base and squeezing gently until she heard him hoarsely cry out her name. His reaction aroused her even more and she licked him all over, sucking the tip while she pumped with her hands and she could feel him getting harder and more heated with every stroke.

Suddenly he grasped her shoulders and moved with amazing dexterity, changing positions so that he was in control, giving her the same treatment she'd given him. His tongue plunged into her sweetness and his mouth devoured her with an urgent suction that sent her right over the edge of passion. Now it was Alexis who was trembling and throbbing and calling his name. It was a long free fall into another world that she never wanted to end. As long as she was in Jared's arms, she'd be happy.

Chapter 7

They made love until Jared became concerned for Alexis's comfort. "I can't have you all sore and gimpy tomorrow. Let's take a shower and I'll make you a meal so good that you'll want to do this again. And again."

Since they were spooned together and he was kissing the nape of her neck between words, Alexis was warm and relaxed and about to disagree with his decision. But once he mentioned food, she realized she was starving. "A perfect idea. Do you want to go first?"

He flipped off the covers and scooped her into his arms. "I want to go together, beauty. It's environmentally sound and erotic at the same time. Besides that, I'll never get enough of seeing you naked."

Alexis was giggling like a schoolgirl when he deposited her in the shower stall. "You're a very strange man," she told him.

By way of response, he cupped her face in his hands and kissed her tenderly. "And I'm all yours, strange ways included." His hands kept moving in circles down her body as he spoke. When he was done she was limp with pleasure from his touch, murmuring his name as he reached his target, the slippery sugar between her legs. He had to support her with one arm as he began to finger her slowly and gently, increasing the pressure and tempo as he slipped his middle finger into her, used his big thumb to stroke her pearl over and over, swallowing her cries of passion into one long, lasting kiss.

When they were finally finished, he rinsed both their bodies clean and wrapped Alexis in a big towel before carrying her back into the bedroom. She rose to a kneeling position and toweled his chest as she asked him to hand her the body lotion. "You don't need this, but I do," she informed him.

"Why wouldn't I need it? White people get ashy, too, beauty. If I don't use lots of moisturizer after every shower I'll look like I've been kickin' flour all day." She was still giggling when they finished rubbing the lightly scented cream into each other's bodies. Now Jared had a choice of putting his dress clothes back on or wearing a towel. He surprised her by opting for a third choice; he went out to his car, shirtless, and came back with a gym bag which contained a change of clothes. He grinned rakishly.

"Never know when you're gonna need fresh attire. Hope your neighbors are all asleep."

"I doubt that, it's not midnight yet. Better hope no one saw you. They'll have the police here in a hot minute," she said.

Jared dressed quickly in jeans, and a long-sleeved striped cotton shirt. "I'm going to investigate your kitchen, if that's okay. What are you hungry for?"

Alexis gave him a wry smile. "Anything. I haven't eaten since breakfast, thanks to you. I'm starving!"

"My apologies, goddess. I'll remedy that in a few minutes."

It took Alexis a while to join him in the kitchen because she just had to tidy up the bathroom and bedroom. She disliked clutter of any kind, and she also wanted to be ready for anything at a moment's notice. Anyone could drop by her home with no warning and find everything spick-and-span, that's just how she was. She changed the sheets, put on a clean duvet cover and made everything look like a photo shoot before she got dressed. After finger-combing her hair into little ringlets, she put on her favorite lounging outfit which consisted of wide-legged yoga pants in a deep rose color and a matching midriff top with a boat neck and long sleeves. Jared was in the kitchen looking through her refrigerator with great concentration when she brought the soiled things to the washer located off the kitchen by the back door.

"Hey, I could have done that," Jared protested at seeing her with the laundry.

"Don't be ridiculous," Alexis answered. "I can do it in like five minutes for one thing, and I'm the clean freak so I get a perverse joy out of doing it, for another. And I'm getting a delightful meal cooked by a handsome man, so I'm getting the best out of the deal if you ask me."

She sat at one of the tall stools by the work island that doubled as a breakfast bar. Jared leaned down and kissed her, a soft, sweet kiss that turned into something more sensual as he sucked gently on her lower lip and pulled it into his mouth. "Alexis, I can't agree with that because I've never had a better time with any woman in my life. You're a very, very special person, beauty." He looked different when he uttered the words. He looked tender and intense and as if he meant every syllable. Alexis had to blink when she saw the expression in his eyes. He changed the subject at once, asking her if there was anything she didn't like to eat.

"Hmm. I'm a pretty good eater. There isn't much I don't like. I don't care for the taste of curry powder, cilantro tastes like soap to me and I love all kinds of lettuce, except iceberg, which gives me a stomachache, and frisée. It's a texture thing," she said with a frown. "It's like getting a mouthful of hair. Yuck."

"And that's why I keep the close shave," Jared muttered. "Anything else I should know about?"

"I hate sweet sauces on fish. I love beets but I can't take the smell of them cooking and I don't like frozen meat. It really creeps me out for some reason." She shuddered, thinking about previous encounters with defrosted steak. "And I can't stand sugar in corn bread. Corn bread should be savory, not sweet."

"You actually have the right idea. Red meat is never as good once it's been frozen. And some people just can't tolerate cilantro—it really does have a nasty taste to them. Your refrigerator is amazing, by the way. Spanking-clean, full of fresh fruit and vegetables, and everything stored properly. That's a nice assortment of cheese and condiments you've got going on there, too. Real Parmigiano-Reggiano and Brie; I'm impressed. You like to cook, don't you?"

"I do," she said. "I like to do almost anything with my hands. I even make jam every year. And liqueurs. Want to try one?"

"Oh my God, I'm in love. A beautiful sexy woman who cooks? Unreal. I'd love to sample something while I'm cooking. How do you feel about spaghetti carbonara?"

"I love it. There's some pancetta in the meat drawer. And some dried porcini mushrooms, if you need them." She poured them each a cordial glass of her peach liqueur, which was praised highly by Jared.

"This is fantastic. Beautiful color and aroma, very peachy taste. You truly are a goddess, Alexis."

She blushed and gave him a kiss that tasted of peaches.

In a very short while, they were dining at the breakfast bar. Jared had made a lovely dish of pasta with chopped pancetta fried crisp, sautéed mushrooms and shallots mixed with beaten eggs and a little cream. A tossed green salad with his herb vinaigrette dressing completed the meal with a glass of the lovely wine he'd brought. They talked quietly while they ate. Jared enjoyed looking at her as they discussed their interests; he loved the way her eyes sparkled and her dimples flashed while she was speaking, and the sexy way her mouth moved while she was eating. Being with her was very relaxing. Her house was as perfect as a very upscale doll house and he told her so.

"Your place is really beautiful. It's not only nice to look at, it's nice to be in. It has a peaceful aura about it. Did you do the decorating?"

"Absolutely, every bit of it. I had to have some things done, like knocking down walls. I took out the dining room walls because they made it too confined. I had the contractors put in the pony wall between the dining room and the kitchen so I could make it into storage. But I did the painting and stuff myself. I'm the queen of bargain shopping so finding the furniture was a lot of fun."

Jared was sipping wine and looking around appreciatively. "You're going to think I'm crazy, but your color scheme reminds me of something unusual."

"Like what?"

"A pistachio," he said sheepishly.

Alexis choked on her wine with a series of ladylike coughs. "But that was my inspiration," she said. "The green in the kitchen, the lavender and purple in the bedroom, the taupe and cream and sage in the living room, all the colors came from picking out all the colors of a pistachio. They're my favorite thing," she said, pointing to a huge glass jar that adorned the dining room table. "One of my favorite things, anyway."

"Aha, I'm learning more about you. You're a woman of exquisite taste, you have an impeccable kitchen and your refrigerator is quite impressive. You have a very eclectic collection of cookbooks, which tells me that you're really interested in food. That alone makes you unique, at least to me. You have two successful businesses. You have a fantastic, open personality and you're possibly the most beautiful woman I've ever been alone with. All I want to do right now is get to know you better."

Alexis could feel a warm peace spread over her at his words. She put her hand on top of his and he turned his hand over so their fingers were entwined. They made a pretty picture, his ivory skin against her rich dark brown. "After I clean the kitchen, I'll tell you anything you want to know. Within reason," she added with a grin.

"I'll clean up," he insisted. "I'm like my dad. I really don't like to see my lady doing grubby housework."

"You're very sweet and old-school, aren't you? But I can do this and, in the meantime, you can go find us some music to put on."

"If you insist. But let's not make this a habit," he said sternly. "You, I intend to spoil so you may as well get used to it."

A little thrill raced down her spine as she looked up at him. He was teasing her, of course, but he sounded so serious she almost believed him. "Just go in the living room and pick out some music. I'll bet you I'll be done with this before you've picked out three CDs."

"You're on."

In about twenty minutes the kitchen was spotless, although it hadn't taken much at all to get it that way. Jared was a very tidy cook and he'd cleaned as he went along, so there was very little to do. She entered the living room bearing a tray that held a bottle of pale green liqueur, two glasses and two glass bowls, one of huge green grapes and one of pistachios. Jared took it from her with a raised eyebrow.

"I could have done that for you."

"Next time you can. Did you find some music?"

"I actually cheated. I put my iPod on your dock over there. I've been looking at your books. You have a very wide range of interests."

Alexis had scooted into her favorite place on the sofa. It was a very pale shade of green with big soft throw pillows in shades of green and purple. It had a chaise that extended on one end and she liked curling up in the corner to read or watch TV. Jared joined her, stretching out on the chaise. The music started playing and Alexis was so startled she jumped.

"What's the matter? Don't you like it?" Jared asked. "It" was *The Way I Feel,* an album of poetry read by Nikki Giovanni with beautiful background music by Arif Mardin. It was recorded in the seventies and it was one of Alexis's very favorite things in the whole world. But how had Jared known that?

"I love it," she said softly. "My aunt BeBe used to play this all the time. BeBe is very funny and avant-garde and she introduced me to a lot of things from what she called her Afro-hippie youth. But how in the world did you know I'd like it?"

Jared gave her a lazy smile. "I told you, I was looking at your books. I saw a lot of poetry books and I saw some Nikki Giovanni so it really wasn't much of a guess on my part. I like poetry, too."

"Who's your favorite poet?"

"Maya Angelou, definitely. But I also like Khalil Gibran, Langston Hughes and e.e. cummings. I like a lot of different poets. I also like songwriters who write poetic lyrics. There's something really unique about a poem that can translate into song."

Alexis felt a tremor of sensation as though her soul had recognized its missing half. Jared was saying things she'd often thought and he was using the same words to describe his feelings. She felt her heart swelling as she carefully phrased her next question. "Which singers do you put in that category?"

"People you probably never heard of," he said with a laugh. "Phoebe Snow, I'm sure you know about her, and Al Jarreau. But there's Laura Nyro, Richie Havens and Kurt Elling. Ever hear of any of them?"

Without a word, Alexis went to the bookcase and took out an album of CDs and brought it to the sofa. She opened it to show Jared every CD Laura Nyro ever made, along with her collection of Phoebe Snow, Richie Havens, Kurt Elling and Steely Dan. "There. How's that for a coincidence?"

Jared sat up with a look of delight on his face. "You're kidding! This is astounding, Alexis. But it's like I told you before, I don't believe in coincidence. I believe in fate, timing and a higher purpose. This is absolutely brilliant," he raved. "How did you find all this great music?" He changed positions so that Alexis was lying on top of him. Her face snuggled into his neck and she felt warm and soft, just perfect. He put his hands on her waist and stroked her back.

Alexis sighed softly. She loved the way his hands felt, the heat that built with every stroke. "My aunt listened to them all the time," she whispered. "We used to sing the songs together and read the lyrics from the liner notes," she murmured. "She had them all on vinyl."

"They were my mom's favorites, and some of my dad's," Jared answered. "Except for Kurt Elling. I started listening to him a few years ago. Great Chicago jazz singer."

"I've seen him in concert," Alexis murmured.

"I'll introduce you," Jared said. "He comes to VanBuren's when he's in Chicago."

Alexis had unbuttoned his shirt and was rubbing his chest with one hand and the sensation was making his body ache. He continued to stroke her body, sliding his hands up to her shoulder blades to discover that she wasn't wearing a bra. He immediately moved his hands to cover her breasts, cupping them and running his thumbs on her hardened nipples over and over until she moaned with desire. The fondling and caressing wasn't enough to appease the heat that was building between them.

He tightened his arms around her and said, "Hold on," while he shifted so that he was sitting up, leaning against the back of the sofa while Alexis was straddling his lap. She rose to her knees and arched her back as he lifted her top and lowered his head to her bare breasts. He started on the left one, tonguing it until it was even harder, and so swollen it was like a ripe blackberry. His eager mouth closed over its sweetness and he sucked it gently at first, then harder, the way she liked it.

Her breath was coming in soft pants and her hands were clutching his shoulders as he pleasured one breast and then the other. Her hips were moving wildly as he continued to drive her crazy with his clever tongue and she buried her hands in his thick hair, holding him in place as the first ripples of completion began between her legs. Jared moved so that she rested on his huge erection and he held her there as his tender torture of her breasts continued. She ground her hips against the weight of his manhood, moaning his name. The ripples turned into one long throbbing release that made her weak from the sheer pleasure he brought to her. He moved his mouth from her breasts to her lips and they joined in a long wet kiss as the waves of release continued to wash over them both.

When the throbbing in her body slowed down to a soft pulsing, Alexis was able to speak again. "Mmm, baby" was all she could manage, but there was a wealth of meaning in the two little words. Jared gave a low, sexy laugh as they held each other tightly.

"I found some protection in my gym bag, if you're interested."

Alexis pulled out of his embrace long enough to put one hand on either side of his face. "I am. But not for a while."

She made a soft sound of surprise as Jared simply stood up with her attached to him. She wrapped her legs around his waist and he carried her into the bedroom and sat down on the side of the bed, which she had already turned down. "Now, what were you saying about not needing protection for a while?"

"You're really strong, aren't you?"

Jared scoffed at her praise. "You're so little I could pick you up with one hand. I'm trying to be careful because I don't want to hurt you," he admitted.

Alexis slipped off her top, proudly showing him the breasts he loved. She gently moved her legs so she could take off her pants.

"I'm indestructible, Jared. You couldn't possibly hurt me. And one of us has on too many clothes," she pointed out.

He remedied that at once, taking off his clothes and lying back on the pile of pillows at the head of the bed. Alexis straddled him again and they kissed, soft and gentle. It got more intense as Alexis sucked his tongue like a lollipop before pulling his lower lip in and treating it to the same delight. The soft suction of her mouth and the feel of her—wet, hot and soft—as she ground her hips against his waiting manhood was too much sensation for Jared. He reached for the condom he'd left on the nightstand and gently broke off the kiss so he could put it on. "Alexis, sweetheart, I find that I'm unable to continue unless I'm buried inside you. I've got to feel all of you right now," he said, his voice husky with need.

Alexis opened her legs wide to accommodate him as he positioned her on his long, thick dick. She held on to his shoulders as he thrust up while she pushed down to take him all the way in. He'd hit the magic spot again on his entry and his sheer size rubbed against her clit every time he moved. When he thrust, she throbbed and with each push into her body, it started the sensation over again. Every erogenous zone on her body was wide-awake and responding to all Jared was giving her. Her vaginal muscles tightened on him and she pumped him harder and harder with every stroke. Her back arched as she squeezed him again; she was trying to give him everything she was getting.

Jared was holding on by a thread. His climax was approaching and he wanted to last longer for Alexis. She leaned back as she moved her supple hips, grinding on him as she rode him. He looked down to see his pole sliding into her tight sweetness and it made him work harder to hold on. Her hot, wet walls clamped down on him and she called his name at the same time and it was all his body needed to explode. Their arms locked around each other, they rode out the storm together until they collapsed, sweaty and satisfied, onto the bed.

Chapter 8

It was about four in the morning before they finally went to sleep. After making more hot, passion-filled love, they showered again and finally consumed some of the grapes and the delectable pistachio liqueur made by Alexis's own hands, while they talked nonstop until they decided that sleep was mandatory. Jared had been assured that the kitchen equipment was coming in the next day and he had to be there to supervise. Their sleep was brief but satisfying. Jared thought he'd get dressed and leave her in bed, but Alexis had other ideas.

"I'm going to the gym. I need a long swim or I won't be able to walk," she said with a smile. "And I need breakfast. I can't function without it."

"Okay, I'll cook something. What sounds good?"

"How about I make something for you? Do you trust me in the kitchen?"

"I trust you with my life, beauty. By the way, you're exceptionally beautiful," he said, draping his arm around her shoulders as they walked to the kitchen. "I've seen you soaking wet by the side of the road, dressed to impress for work, dolled up to enchant in that fabulous red number. And now I've seen you first thing in the morning—without any of the totally unnecessary makeup you wear so well—and I've reached the conclusion that you are the most gorgeous woman I've ever had the pleasure to know."

Alexis burst into laughter. "Thank you, Jared. That was a sweet thing to say. Very poetic, actually."

"I used to write poetry," he admitted. "I actually won a few awards for my writing."

Alexis tried not to let her face show what she was thinking as she took a box of steel-cut oats out of the cabinet. "You are versatile, indeed. Would you like coffee?"

"Yes, and I'll make it. It's the least I can do," he said, reaching for the French press and the coffee grinder.

Alexis quickly prepared the oatmeal, crisp bacon, English muffins and eggs over easy. Jared was totally knocked out by the homemade plum preserves she served with the muffins.

"You have a real gift for this," he said. "This is like a lost art. Besides my gran and my mom, I don't know anyone else who still does this."

"Well, folks don't have to do it anymore," Alexis said. "It used to be a way of life but now you can just go to the store and get a jar of jam, so most people don't take the time to do it."

"Most of the commercial stuff is full of preservatives and tastes like crap. This tastes like plums."

His cell phone played its tune and he glanced at the caller ID. Apologizing, he took the call, walking into the dining room. The doorbell rang at the same time, and Alexis tightened the belt on her pink robe as she went to see who in the world could be calling at such an ungodly hour. She opened the door to find someone she'd known for years, a woman named Karen Johnson. Alexis's surprise showed on her face as she greeted her visitor.

"Hello, Karen. How can I help you this morning?"

The other woman grinned and flipped back her long extension braids. "Hello, Alexis. I forgot you lived around here. I'm here on business, actually. You know I'm a detective with the Columbia P.D. and I'm following up on a few calls we got last night about a prowler in the neighborhood."

"A prowler! It's so quiet in this subdivision, I don't think anything like that has happened since I moved here."

"That's why we're checking it out. We got three calls reporting a white man breaking into a car. One caller said he was naked, which seems highly unlikely in November." She chuckled. "It was after midnight when the calls came in and I wanted to warn you that someone could be on the prowl, and to ask if you heard anything strange last night."

Alexis shook her head as she tried to remember. "Everything was normal around here last night, Karen. I can't imagine what your callers thought they saw, but nothing happened here."

No sooner were the words out of her mouth than Jared appeared in the foyer next to her. "Listen, beauty, I've got to run. That call was from the delivery driver and I've got to meet him in about thirty… Oh, I'm sorry, I didn't mean to interrupt," he apologized. "I'm Jared VanBuren," he added, shaking Karen's hand. "I'll call you this afternoon," he said to Alexis as he kissed her goodbye.

Karen's light brown face was red across her cheekbones and she looked stunned as she watched Jared go down the front walk to his Range Rover. She finally tore her eyes away from him and fixed Alexis with an expression of pure incredulity. "Girl, I'm scared of you," she said with wonder. "So nothing out of the ordinary happened here last night, huh?"

* * *

Sherri's eyes brightened at the sight of Alexis entering her office with a covered basket. "Bless your heart, you brought me lunch! I can't thank you enough because I was going to have to grab something on the way to the hospital. What did you bring me?"

Alexis sighed deeply as she unpacked the basket, which contained a turkey sandwich on rye, a mixed green salad and a big Fuji apple pear along with a bunch of grapes, a couple homemade brownies and an ice-cold bottle of green tea. "Here ya go," she said glumly.

"Yum! You're a lifesaver, sister. I'll be right back."

When she returned to the office, which was decorated in soothing earth tones, Alexis had taken off her coat and was curled up in a corner of the small sofa with a gloomy countenance.

"What's the matter? You look like someone stole your puppy, chick. What happened with that big gorgeous Samaritan from yesterday? I tried to call you about a zillion times and I kept going right to voice mail," Sherri said before taking a big bite of the sandwich.

"I had the phone turned off. I was busy. Really, really busy."

"Busy with what?"

"Oh, doing something incredibly reckless, something I've never even contemplated in my entire life. And I mean never—not even once," Alexis said dramatically.

Sherri took a swallow of tea and popped a grape in her mouth. "Alexis, sweetie, we can do the long version tonight but I only have another thirty-five minutes before I need to be making rounds. So cut to the proverbial chase, please. Don't make me beat it out of you."

Alexis took a deep breath and began, "I went to Jared's loft yesterday morning so I could pick him up to take him to his car." Speaking in a rapid, expressionless voice she gave her friend a truncated, PG version of what had occurred during her momentous day and had the dubious pleasure of watching Sherri's face go from mildly interested to amused to surprised to absolutely delighted. When she finished her recitation, Alexis was looking quite grumpy and she ended it by saying, "And it's mostly your fault, too."

"My fault? What did I do?"

Alexis triumphantly whipped out a piece of paper from the pocket of her trousers, which was neatly folded but bore the unmistakable look of having been read many times. Wordlessly she handed it to Sherri like a summons.

Sherri opened it and began studying it carefully, then grinned as she recognized it for what it was—Alexis's wish list.

"Okay, well, I get it. Jared fits most of these, I can see that. What are the question marks for at the bottom?"

Alexis was now walking around the office with her arms crossed. "Remember the one thing you told me to put on the list, my big secret desire that no one else would know, ever?"

Sherri nodded as she chewed another bite of turkey on rye.

"That secret thing was poetry," Alexis said simply. "I wanted a man who liked poetry as much as I do, someone who had a real appreciation of the art. Last night when Jared came to pick me up for dinner, I had on a red dress."

"The jersey dress with the wrap in front? That looks stupendous on you."

"Sherri, focus! I open the door and he's standing there with red roses and wine. And then he puts down the wine and roses and takes my hands and recites Langston Hughes's poem, 'When Sue Wears Red.'"

"Ohhh, Alexis," Sherri said breathlessly. "Did he really?"

"Yeah, really."

"So that's why you two ended up getting all busy and

spending the night together," she said. "Not to mention the fact that he looks at you like…"

"Like what?"

"Like you're the most beautiful thing he's ever seen in his life."

Alexis stopped walking and stared at Sherri. "He said that this morning," she confessed.

"So why are you looking so depressed? It's not every day that you meet your soul mate, so why aren't you happy? Did he leave you in the middle of the night or something?" Her eyes narrowed as though she was getting ready for a fight, which she was. If he'd tried to hurt Alexis, Jared VanBuren would indeed have a battle on his hands.

"No, he left in the morning. After the police came to tell me a naked white man was seen trying to break into a car near my house."

"The *police?*" Sherri was plainly appalled.

"Oh, not just the police. Karen Johnson showed up at my door and dropped her little bomb right before Jared walked up, said he had to meet a deliveryman at the restaurant and kissed me goodbye. Did you know she was a detective?"

"It's a good fit," Sherri said. "She was always the nosiest girl in school. What did she say?"

"The usual mess about 'Girl, I'm scared of you' and 'I didn't think you were the type to cross over all the lovely.' Things we say to each other when we're being nice-nasty and all up in each other's business. I didn't tell her that Jared really had been out to his car with no shirt on. He's not modest at all and the cold doesn't bother him. He's from Chicago and he thinks it's warm down here." Alexis stopped pacing for a minute, fingering one of her silver hoop earrings with one hand and shoving her other hand into her pocket.

"So someone did see a naked white man in the neighborhood. Well, partially naked, anyway. So what? Probably did somebody good to see that gorgeous body of his. And who cares what Karen Johnson thinks? She's always been kind of a heifer, if you ask me, and it's not like she's your friend or anything," Sherri said bracingly.

"Yeah, well she's not the only one with an opinion. My merry group of minions at Sanctuary wasn't much better than Karen the cop. As soon as I walked in I got a chorus of 'oohs' and 'aahs' and some applause because there was a huge flowering plant waiting for me from Jared. And also because I wore my 'glow of satisfaction' so well, this according to Javier. They all saw him with me there yesterday so, of course, their filthy minds jumped to conclusions. Little monsters," she said wryly. She tried to suppress a self-deprecating grin, but there was a definite hint of amusement in her voice.

Sherri had to cover her mouth to keep from laughing because Alexis did have the unmistakable glow of a satisfied woman. She was wearing a pair of slim-fitting wool slacks in a pale blue-gray with a matching silk shirt and her usual high heels, ankle boots this time, in deference to the crisp weather. To anyone who knew her well, it was easy to see that something was up; it was as if she was radiating light from inside.

"Even Javier turned on you? That's hard to believe. He's Mr. Loyalty, and he always has your back."

Alexis raised the corner of her upper lip in a dainty sneer. "Of course he didn't say anything in front of anyone. He has way too much class for that. He waited until I was in the office and then he pounced. And to think I was gonna promote him!"

"You'll still give him his due. He's just happy for you, like I am. And yes, I'm very happy because this is exactly what you wanted and what you need and deserve. What did Ava say?"

Alexis dropped her head and waved a hand like she was testifying in church. "Thank the Father she didn't utter a word because she's about a hair away from unemployment, but you know she can't keep anything to herself. By now the whole family knows I was, umm, well, whatever they think I was up to. I'm not ready to deal with this, I'm really not."

Sherri glanced at her watch and made a sound of exasperation. "Listen, Lexie, I don't want to leave you in your time of need, but I've got to get to the hospital. What are you doing after work?"

"Hiding out, probably. Can I come and hide at your house?"

"Why would you want to do that? What's the matter with you? Jared is just lovely, if you ask me. He's got every single attribute on your list—well, except for *that* one—and a whole lot more. He's your Poetry Man," she warbled in a campy imitation of Phoebe Snow.

Alexis was pacing again but she stopped long enough to reach into her bra and pull out a folded piece of paper and handed it to Sherri. "You don't know the half of it," she muttered. "He wrote me a poem before he left this morning."

Sherri looked thrilled. "Girl, I think you found your man," she murmured as she looked at the words he'd written.

"Yeah, but I was looking for Mr. Right, not Mr. White."

"The devil is a liar," Sherri said hotly. "You take that back. You know damned well you didn't mean that. Maybe you'd better haul yourself in for some serious talk because I can see that you're a little overwrought, to say the least. I have patients. Thanks for lunch, I'll see you later." Sherri hugged her hard and grabbed her coat and satchel before blazing out the door. Of course she had to have the last word, though. "But I notice you kept that poem tucked right next to your heart, didn't you, Lexie? Don't ever give me anything out of your tits again unless it's cash. Bye!"

Alexis, despite her angst, had to laugh at that exit line.

Chapter 9

Jared surveyed the restaurant kitchen with approval. It had taken all day, but the custom equipment was finally in. There was nothing quite like the sight of a brand-new virgin kitchen to get a chef's passion flowing and excite his imagination and Jared was no exception. He ran his hands over the sleek cool stainless steel of the walk-in refrigerators and looked in the ovens, inspecting them all—the wood-fired one for pizza, the salamander for quick browning and the huge gas ovens for regular roasting and baking. Usually his initial thoughts in a new kitchen centered on the first meal he'd cook there, but all he could think about was showing it off to Alexis. He left the kitchen to look at the dining room again.

It was almost finished and it looked great so far. The floors were hardwood, in a dark espresso-brown shade that would match the chairs and tables. Right now the expensive flooring was underneath a thick paper covering to protect them until the walls were finished. The interior walls were being covered with slate tiles. The natural color of the slate was steel-blue with gray, charcoal and copper striations that gave them a rich depth and beauty. A dark gray wainscoting surrounded the main dining room. The bar area was tiled from floor to ceiling in glass subway tiles the same color as the ocean on a stormy day. Custom light fixtures made of copper with frosted glass globes hung over the bar's granite top. The main dining room was lit with high-hat ceiling lights as well as wall sconces made of copper and teak with opaline glass. There were two private dining rooms, both of which were papered with dark blue silk shantung wallpaper. His younger sister did the designing for all of his restaurants and her excellent taste showed.

He was hoping for a soft opening in three weeks, but it wasn't etched in stone; too many little things could go awry and delay the finish of the project and Jared never opened the doors to the public until everything was perfect. Right now the potential delays were in the foyer, where a waterfall was supposed to be installed. Rough natural granite slabs were being put in and the water was supposed to trickle down continuously with a circulating pump. The tables and chairs were being custom made in Washington state and they were already two days late in arriving. Jared frowned, knowing that he'd have to put in a call to his sister that night. But right now, he was calling his goddess, Alexis.

A slight frisson of sensation went down his back when he heard her voice. He'd been experiencing little aftershocks all day and he enjoyed it. Lovemaking like theirs deserved encores.

"Hello, beauty. How's my fiancée today?"

"Very funny. You need to stop doing that." Alexis sounded amused, which gave him no reason to stop, but he kept that to himself.

"Listen, I'm filthy from head to toe and I need to get

cleaned up before I go out into polite society. But once I do, I was hoping I could persuade you to come to work with me."

"Do what? I thought you'd worked at the restaurant all day. What else do you have to do there?"

"Aah, but this is a different kind of work. I always check out the competitors when I move into a new area. I go to all the upscale restaurants to see what I'm up against, and since I owe you a nice meal in a nice restaurant, I'd love to have your company."

He could almost see her face as she answered him. "So this is strictly business, is that right?"

He imagined her giving him a slight side eye with the perfectly arched brow over her left eye raised just so and the mental picture was totally adorable. "No, it's not strictly business. It's barely business at all. I can't stand being away from you. Yesterday was the best day of my life and I want to pick up where we left off. Am I wrong in thinking that you were enjoying my company?"

"Of course not, but I can't make it. Thanks for asking," she added.

"Are you busy all night? The place I had in mind is open late," he said in his best voice of persuasion.

"Well, no, I'm not, but I have an errand to run for my mother."

"I'll help you," he said. "I'd like to meet your mother, anyway. Think she'll like me?"

"You won't get to meet her tonight. She's on a Caribbean cruise but I have to take care of some things for her because she can't rely on Ava to remember anything she's supposed to do."

"Ava will never learn responsibility if no one gives her any. Oprah said that on her show the other day. Or maybe it was Dr. Phil. Come to think of it, my mom says it all the time or she used to when I was a feckless adolescent." He was pleased to hear her giggling and he pushed his advantage.

"Since you can't reeducate your sibling in one evening, it will be my pleasure to assist you in your tasks and then take you out for a meal that won't be as good as what you'll get at Seven-Seventeen, but the conversation will be great. How does that sound?"

"It sounds rather nice, but I still don't need your help. It's very sweet of you to offer, but I can handle it. How about I meet you there? Does that work for you?"

"Just barely," he said. "I personally like to pick up my lady at her door and escort her to wherever we're going. Anything else is uncivilized and ungentlemanly."

"You really sound old-school," Alexis teased him.

"Totally. I was raised to be a gentleman in a world full of scoundrels and I'll tell you all about it over dinner."

She giggled again and it sent another sweet aftershock through him. He gave her the name of the restaurant and said he'd meet her there at eight. He ran his hand over his chin and winced when he felt the stubble. He decided he'd take extra time getting ready so that he'd look his absolute best for her. He'd just met her, but he was already willing to do anything it took to please her in every way possible.

Alexis really did have to do a few things for her mother. With her out of town, it was entirely possible that Ava would let the house burn to the ground. The first thing she did was pick up her mother's Yorkie from the boarders. There was no way on earth that her mother would have left her precious pup in Ava's care, so she'd had her boarded for the week. Her mom would be back the next day and the doggy hotel would be closed by the time she landed at the airport, so Sparkle had to be fetched that evening. The little dog was thrilled to see Alexis and she yipped and yapped her happiness most of the way home.

When they reach her mother's neat ranch-style house, Alexis was immediately ticked off at Ava's typical irresponsibility. The mailbox was full, the newspapers were still on the porch and two big black trash bags were on the back stoop instead of in the garage bins where they belonged. The inside of the house was worse; Ava's belongings started at the back door and were everywhere. Shoes in the kitchen, two jackets tossed on the counter, three purses hanging from the backs of chairs, and that was just the kitchen. Clean clothes were exploding out of the washer, or maybe they were dirty? Alexis wasn't about to investigate them to find out.

One end of the dining room had been covered with a thick towel and used as an ironing board and the other end was evidently a makeup station, judging by the big mirror and array of cosmetics scattered about. There were more shoes in the living room, along with every outfit Ava had worn that week, tossed all over her mother's tasteful and expensive furniture. The television was on in the family room and Alexis and Sparkle followed the sound, expecting to find Ava and give her a stern lecture. But Ava was nowhere to be found. The nitwit had gone off and left the TV on, as well as the computer and several lights. Alexis's cheeks filled up with air that she blew out noisily; she was mad enough to spit.

"Sparkle, we've got to get busy. There's no way I can leave this place looking like a flophouse. I'm gonna hand that sorry wench her head the next time I see her."

Apparently Sparkle agreed with her because she was growling at an expensive-looking blouse that was hanging over the side of a chair. Muttering unladylike words under her breath, Alexis set to work. In less than an hour she had the house looking neat as a pin by the simple expedient of putting everything that was out of place into large trash bags and tossing them into Alexis's room. After getting one glimpse of the disaster that was her sister's bedroom, she shuddered and closed the door firmly.

"I can't believe a sister of mine lives like this. Something really needs to be done about her," she said aloud as she got out the things she needed to give everything a good dusting. She followed that up by running the vacuum and cleaning the kitchen a bit. That didn't take very long because Ava had been eating out to judge by the number of takeout containers and soda cups all over the family room. "That's another reason she's always broke. She wastes money going out to eat instead of taking twenty minutes to make a decent meal."

Thinking about meals made her remember her date and she prepared to leave the house, but not before feeding Sparkle. Of course, there was no dog food; Ava was too trifling to go to the grocery store as her mother had asked. The note was still on the refrigerator with the grocery list, but Alexis would bet anything that Ava had spent the money her mother had left. What a gal.

"Okay, chick, you're coming with me. I can't leave you here to starve. But you must behave because I have a date and I'm going to leave you alone for a while."

Sparkle didn't seem to mind the news; when Alexis picked her up, she made a game attempt to lick her face. "Don't go there, sweetie. Nobody kisses me in the face except Jared." Alexis stopped dead in her tracks, stunned by how easily that had slipped out. For a moment she felt like a child who'd stepped into the deep end of the pool with no warning. This date could be just as unsettling and just as dangerous, if she wasn't on her guard. She and Sparkle got in the car and she headed for home to get ready.

Alexis felt much better after a hot shower and she decided she looked fabulous considering that she only had an hour to get ready for her date. She decided on black wool slacks with a bit of stretch that gave them a nice close fit and showed off her butt really well. With it she wore a deep rose cashmere sweater with a cropped waist and a ruched neck. She had on gold stick earrings with a small diamond at both the lobe and the end, plus her charm bracelet. The earrings drew the eye to her face and the bracelet looked feminine and sentimental but chic against her perfectly manicured hand. A quick spray of Trésor Midnight Rose and she was done, right down to her Louboutin pumps. She slipped on a black tailored coat in cashmere and gave Sparkle a little talk before she left.

"I won't be gone very long, cutie. Be a good girl and don't poop on anything, okay?"

Curled up on a soft fluffy pillow, Sparkle gave a little bark that could have meant that she agreed or it could have meant the opposite. Alexis would find out in a few hours.

After all the trouble she'd gone to, Alexis wasn't thrilled with her date so far. The Brasserie was a nice place. She'd actually eaten there once or twice, but she didn't remember the service being so poor on her previous visits. The hostess, a leggy blonde with extensions that came almost to her waist, offered to seat her and Alexis told her that she was meeting Mr. VanBuren. He wasn't there, the hostess informed her, but she took her to a table set for two. Alexis ordered a glass of wine and waited for Jared. And waited some more. She was getting hungry and she was also getting annoyed. Punctuality was something she insisted on in her associations. She was always on time and she saw no reason why she shouldn't expect the same from her employees, her clients and certainly her dates, particularly Jared since he'd been on time yesterday. It was bad enough when she had to waste time waiting on her perpetually tardy sister or her mother, who also had a tendency to disregard time, but sitting around in a restaurant waiting for a man who didn't have the decency to keep a date was just galling.

It was an upscale place, nicely decorated with a warm ambience, but it was full of couples, which only served to underscore the fact that she was apparently being stood up. The next time the server came by she was going to ask for the check and leave, she decided. She checked the time again and realized that she'd been waiting for thirty minutes. At least he could have had the decency to call, she thought as her anger mounted. Just then her phone, which was on the table next to her rapidly drumming fingers, began to vibrate. She answered it in a barely civil tone of voice.

"Hello?"

"Alexis, is something wrong? Did you change your mind or are you having a hard time finding the place or what?"

"What are you talking about?"

"I've been waiting here at the restaurant for forty-five minutes and I got concerned, that's all. If you can't make it…"

She cut him off in midsentence. "Jared, what are you talking about? I've been here for a half hour waiting for you!"

"You what? Where are you?"

She told him and he was at her table in less than a minute. He did not look amused. The hostess came over and asked if she could help.

"No, you've done quite enough for tonight," Jared said in a tight, measured voice that let anyone within earshot know that he was angry. "When I came here tonight, what did I tell you?"

The hostess flipped her ridiculous hair over her shoulder as she gulped out an answer. "That your name was Jared Van-Buren and that a lady would be joining you."

"Good, you remembered. So when my lady arrived, why did you tell her that I wasn't here and seat her all the way across the dining room? Is that the way you handle your guests?"

"Umm, aah, no," she stammered.

"Then may I ask why you felt it was an appropriate procedure for me and my lady?"

The hostess had turned bright red and her face was covered in perspiration. Jared hadn't raised his voice; on the contrary, he was being exceedingly polite, which made everything seem much worse. By now the owner of the restaurant had been alerted that something was amiss and he came to the table to find out what was wrong. He recognized Jared on sight and greeted him warmly.

"Jared, I'd heard you were in town. Why didn't you let me know you were coming?"

"That may have been a good idea, Sam. If I had, I might not be having this conversation with your employee. I made a reservation under my name and when I arrived, I let her know that I was expecting a lady who would ask for me by name. She did so and was told I wasn't here. She's been sitting over here waiting for me for thirty minutes while I've been on the other side of the room waiting for her. I'm having a real problem with that, Sam."

Sam Lamsey, the owner, was also turning red as Jared explained the situation. He looked at the hostess, Kayla, and waited for her version of events.

"When she came in, she asked for Mr. VanBuren and I figured she meant another Mr. VanBuren because, umm, because, well, I just assumed she meant someone else and I seated her so that when her Mr. VanBuren got here..."

Jared cut in, using an icy voice that Alexis would have never credited to him. "Her Mr. VanBuren was already here, waiting very impatiently for her," he said, putting his hand over Alexis's. "I'm not going to ask why you didn't at least inquire if I was the right man because your reasoning is painfully obvious. I would suggest, Sam, that you consider some retraining for your front-of-the-house staff."

Kayla's face worked frantically as she tried to decide what to say next, but Sam wisely sent her to take a break before she burst into loud tears, which looked like her next move. He bowed to Alexis and issued a very sincere apology.

"Miss, I truly apologize for any inconvenience or discomfort afforded you this evening. It's never our intention to offer anything but the finest hospitality in Columbia to all of our patrons. Jared, I also extend an apology to you. I assure you that Kayla—and all her counterparts—will be getting some training that is much needed in view of tonight's stupidity. Of course, your dinner is on me, if you'll allow me to serve you personally."

It was a really nice apology, but Jared wasn't having it. "Sam, thanks for the offer, but we're going to be leaving. You're a married man and I'm pretty sure that, if you felt your wife had been insulted, you'd want to take her home and make her feel better. And that's what I'm going to do now." He rose, standing several inches taller than the older man. He shook his hand, even as Sam Lamsey continued to express his sadness at the situation and offer them anything in the house, anytime at all.

Jared was helping Alexis put on her coat as he made his parting statement. "I appreciate the offer and maybe we'll take you up on it one day, but right now—" he smiled down at Alexis "—I'm taking my lady home."

Chapter 10

Alexis hadn't said a word during the entire episode, but once they were in the parking lot she found her voice. "Jared, that was a little intense, don't you think?"

Jared squeezed the hand he was holding and looked down at her. "Not intense enough, actually, but I didn't want to make a scene. I'm still hungry and I'm sure you haven't eaten since breakfast. Where would you like to go?"

"To tell you the truth, I'd just like to go home." She explained about her overnight guest, ending by saying, "I just hate to leave her alone in a relatively strange place."

They'd reached her car and Jared took her keys to unlock the door. He opened the door for her and said, "That's no problem. I'll get takeout for us and meet you there. I'm going to follow you home first, and make sure you get in safely."

She smiled up at him. He was the most protective man she'd ever met, even when she didn't need protecting. "Jared, I'll be fine. I'll see you in a bit."

Sparkle was abundantly glad to have her home, demonstrating her joy by dancing around in circles. Alexis scooped her up and let her give her a quick lick on the nose. "Okay, little girl. Calm down, we're going to have company. I need to change clothes and we're gonna get ready for him. How does that sound?"

By the time Jared arrived with a bag of takeout from a restaurant that specialized in low-country cooking, everything was ready. Alexis had started a fire in the fireplace and put a blanket on the floor with several big pillows. She'd pulled over the coffee table next to the blanket and arranged plates, flatware and glasses on top, along with a bottle of wine. She'd changed into a pair of cream-colored leggings with a loose-fitting top. Jared put the bag on the table and Alexis took his coat. He squatted down to greet Sparkle, who was hiding behind Alexis.

"Hello, Miss Sparkle. You aren't scared of me, are you? I like little dogs," he said soothingly. His voice worked like a charm and she trotted over to him with a wagging tail and a happy doggie smile. He sat on the floor and played with her while Alexis washed her hands and put the food on their plates.

"You've won her heart, Jared. That's surprising because she's really shy around men."

Jared finally stood and went to the kitchen to wash his hands. Sparkle followed him, running to keep up with his long legs. "She doesn't like men? Couldn't tell it by me."

"She's not used to being around men. The only man she sees on a regular basis is my father, and she adores him. But other than that, she's around my mom and my sisters and that's it."

They dined on succulent roast chicken, string beans and small red-skinned potatoes with spinach salad. Jared fed Sparkle tiny bits of chicken and she was in heaven.

Jared looked curious. "I hate to be nosy, but I thought you said your parents are divorced."

"They are," Alexis assured him. "But I'm ninety-nine-percent positive that they still date. Daddy is a college professor. He used to teach at the University of South Carolina, here in Columbia. But after they divorced, he moved to Savannah and he teaches there. We see him every few weeks but somehow he and Sparkle have formed a bond." She laughed merrily.

"One day Daddy was in town and he and I went over to Mama's to pick up Ava for lunch. Well, Miss Sparkle went flying to him and jumped all over his feet until he picked her up and gave her some attention. That could only happen if she'd been around him fairly often, so he must be seeing Mama a lot more often than we suspected. They're very sneaky about it because they don't want anyone to know, at least my mother doesn't. But Mama's not as slick as she thinks she is. I figured it out a long time ago."

"Seriously? Why don't they get remarried if they still care for each other?"

"It might be because Mama never likes to admit she's wrong. She thought Daddy was cheating on her and that was it as far as she was concerned. She went charging ahead with the divorce because of the so-called family curse. My mother and my grandmother and my aunts are some of the sweetest people you'll ever meet, but they're nuts. They're convinced that all of the women in our family are doomed to have miserable relationships with men. No woman in this family has ever had a happy marriage and according to my grandmother, none of us ever will."

"Do you believe that?

"Oh, I think it's just garbage because it isn't true. There are happy marriages in this family. People just conveniently forget about them when they're trying to make a point so you can't convince them that the whole thing is just a bunch of hoo-ha. I think that's why Mama is keeping her relationship with Daddy a big secret, because she doesn't want to have to listen to a lot of foolishness from her family. It's crazy, it really is." She sighed.

Jared leaned across the table and kissed her. "Everybody's family is a little bit nuts in one way or another. I'm just glad you don't buy into the whole curse thing. That would mean we're doomed from the start and nothing could be further from the truth." He kissed her again to underscore his declaration.

Alexis insisted on helping him clear things out of the living room, although he washed the dishes. She perched on a stool and watched him quickly dispatch the few dishes they'd used. She liked looking at him; he was undeniably handsome. But he was also quite surprising as she'd seen at the restaurant.

"Jared, you were pretty upset tonight," she began.

"I wasn't upset, Alexis, I was furious. If that had happened at one of my places, that little twit would have been fired on the spot. What she did was stupid, disrespectful and ignorant. You have to understand that nobody disrespects you and gets away with it, especially when I'm right there. That's just not gonna happen." He spoke quietly but with utter assurance. "You can't tell me that you were okay with the way she treated you. I just won't believe it."

"Of course I wasn't happy with it, not in the least. I was having a little fantasy about her extensions getting ripped out one at a time, to tell you the truth. But unfortunately, I've had a lifetime to get used to people's small minds and their prejudice. At first I thought that you were late, or you were standing me up for some reason. I didn't think anything else. I was just getting really annoyed with you," she admitted.

"Then you called me and you showed up at my table and

I finally knew what had been going on, and yes, I got mad. But not as mad as you did," she said demurely.

"Alexis, a hostess has one job and that is to display perfect hospitality to all guests by paying attention to the details that encompass their presence in the restaurant, okay? It shouldn't have taken her thirty seconds to bring you to the right table once you said you were meeting me. Instead, she just assumes that you're meeting someone else and drags you off across the dining room to some dark corner. If she'd done her job correctly, that wouldn't have happened. But she didn't do her job correctly because of some stupid inbred idea about matching people up by the color of their hair or their skin or something. That and the fact that she was in my face every ten minutes throwing that horsehair around and jiggling those plastic boobs like they're a big prize. Flaming idiot."

Jared finished the kitchen and came around to her side of the counter and took her hands, leading her over to the blanket. He sat first, pulling her down so that she was between his long legs with her back resting on his chest. Sparkle ran over to them with her tail going like mad, but she waited for an invitation before getting in Alexis's lap. Jared held Alexis close and rubbed his face against her neck, inhaling her sexy fragrance.

"Jared, one of the realities of dating someone from another race is that there's always going to be someone with something to say about it. Most people don't pay it any attention, but some people do. And we're in the Deep South, too. Some old attitudes die really hard."

He took his time responding because he was kissing her neck and licking her ear. "A lot of things have changed, Alexis. There're always going to be jerks but that doesn't mean we have to put up with it. Nothing and no one is going to bother you as long as I'm breathing and that's a promise."

She turned her head so that he had better access to the sensitive spots on the side of her face and her neck. "That's good to know, especially since the cops were here this morning to follow up on reports of a naked white man breaking into a car. Next time I'll let you handle it," she said with a soft laugh.

That broke his concentration and he gently turned her face so that he could see her better. "Are you kidding? When were they here?"

"The woman you introduced yourself to as you were leaving is a detective who was asking questions and informing the neighborhood about a prowler. A naked prowler," she added with a mischievous grin.

"I'm sorry, beauty. I'll go to the police station and explain tomorrow morning. I don't want your neighbors to think they're under attack from some random crazy man."

"You don't have to do that. It would only cause more confusion, trust me. This is an established neighborhood with a lot of retired people and older married couples. I bought a house here because it was a good price and it was a nice, safe area. But being a young single woman makes me an object of great interest to some people. Some really nosy people who live for gossip," she said with a slight shake of her head.

"This puts me in an awkward position," Jared said ruefully. "On the one hand, I don't want to scandalize the neighbors and make you look like a scarlet woman, but on the other hand, I hadn't planned on skulking off in the middle of the night, either."

Alexis picked up Sparkle and turned around completely so that she could give him a kiss. "I can help you with that, sweetie. I don't want you to leave and I don't really care what the neighbors think. But I do think you should keep all your clothes on if you have to go outside."

Jared smiled, the sexy, loving smile she recognized from the day before. "I think I can manage that, as long as I can take off all my clothes in here."

"That depends on how fast you can and what you do when you're naked."

"If that's the case, I can show you better than I can tell you." He stood up and held out his hands to her. "Come with me, goddess."

Chapter 11

After putting out the fire and making Sparkle comfortable on a pillow next to the fireplace, Jared put his arms around Alexis and she wrapped her legs about his waist as he walked her into the bedroom. His mouth closed over hers and his tongue found hers, mating with each other as their twin passions began to mount. He slowly released her and placed her on the bed before stripping off the crewneck merino wool sweater that matched his eyes. He tossed it over his shoulder and showed off his hard-muscled chest as he sat down to take off his shoes, socks and pants.

"Totally unclothed, as requested. Now it's your turn," he said seductively.

Alexis rose to her knees to begin her own striptease, but Jared was on his knees, too, helping her remove each item. Her soft, loose-fitting top came off quickly, followed by an alluring half-cup bra. His lips covered one of her nipples and his tongue teased it into a hard peak of arousal while his hands stroked her leggings and thong off as if he was peeling a ripe banana. In seconds she was as naked as he was and just as ready for love. This time it was both wilder and sweeter than the night before because they were familiar with each other's bodies and they knew how to please each other.

His hands knew just how to touch her, and where and how long. His tongue lavished her breasts, filling her with a hot yearning for more. He licked a path of fire down her flat, firm stomach to her navel and she discovered that it was an erogenous zone, too. The tip of his tongue circled it and went in and out as he treated it to the same kind of kiss he'd put on her lips. She felt the beginning of her first release as he moved down to her sweet spot, using his fingers to enter her and his mouth to bring her to a shattering climax that went on and on as her hands clutched the sheets. She was still throbbing and gasping from his loving assault on her body when he finally slowed down.

She relaxed against his warm body as he held her close and kissed her again and again, until she was ready for more. This time she put the condom on him and when he was sheathed they joined their bodies hard and fast. He was on top of her and their bodies moved as one, pumping and thrusting until they came together and collapsed, trembling and breathing hard. He rolled over on his back and they held each other as their heartbeats gradually returned to normal. When they were able to talk again, Alexis murmured, "Jared, that was, mmm."

He whispered back, "Yes, it was, baby. It really was." Those were the last words they spoke before falling into a deep, satisfied sleep.

Jared came awake slowly, his arms around Alexis as they lay spooned together. He kissed the back of her neck and rubbed his cheek against her soft hair. "How would you like to go away for the weekend?"

Alexis yawned sleepily. "Go where?"

"I need to go to Hilton Head. I'm looking for some property there. A restaurant and a house," he said. "I've been talking with a Realtor and he's got some places for me to see. Would you like to come with me?"

Alexis didn't hesitate, she said yes at once. "That sounds like fun."

"That's great, Alexis. I'll make us a hotel reservation right now."

She turned so that she was facing him and smiled. "Actually, we don't need one. My best friend's family has a vacation house there and I have the keys. It's really nice, you'll love it."

"Anyplace you are, I'll love. What's on your planner for today?"

"Everything." She sighed. "Work, teaching water aerobics and returning Sparkle to her mommy. It's not too bad, really. How about you?"

"I'll be trying to find out where my chairs and tables are, meeting with suppliers and overseeing the crew at Seven-Seventeen. A long day."

"Sounds like it. Then we should be getting up and out right about now," Alexis said.

"You're right, we should. And we will, in just a few minutes," he answered as he turned on his side to face her.

It was more than a few minutes before they actually made it to the shower, but they put the time to very good use.

Alexis looked over at Sparkle who was bouncing on the car seat with joy. She'd had a wonderful day, going to the spa with Alexis where she was doted on by everyone. Alexis had taken her to the health club and the manager had gladly babysat her during the water aerobics class. And now they were turning into the driveway of her mommy's house and she was excited. Alexis, not so much.

"I'd give a lot to know how you know where you are. You can barely see out of the window." She drove as slowly as possible, trying to think of a way to make a hasty exit. "Maybe I can drop you on the porch, ring the bell and run. Is that a plan?"

Sparkle barked loudly, which Alexis interpreted as a no. "Fine. But I'm not going to be responsible for whatever happens once we're in there."

She parked the car and picked up the wiggly little dog. As they were walking to the front door, it was opened wide by her mother.

"There's my little girl! Did you miss me?"

Alexis put down Sparkle and she began to dance, spinning around in circles to show how happy she was to be back at home. Thinking she could sneak away fast, Alexis said, "Good to see you, Mama. Did you have a good time? Well, I've got to run, so I'll call you later." She whirled around and her foot was actually on the top step when her mother's voice froze her in her tracks.

"You didn't think it would be that easy, did you? Turn yourself around and come right on in. What's this I hear about you and some strange man?"

Her sisters had big mouths. Either Ava or Alana had mentioned that Alexis had met a man. A sigh that started at her toes worked its way up through her body and made its escape through her lips. There was no escaping the inevitable so she may as well get it over with now. She put a reasonable approximation of a sunny smile on her face as she turned to face her mother, the one and only Aretha Sharp.

Fabulous was the only word to adequately describe Aretha. It was an often overused term, but nothing else fit the bill so well. She was petite and shapely and it was easy to see where

Alexis and her sisters got their good looks. Her chocolate-brown skin was smooth and devoid of any lines whatsoever. Her thick hair was short and chic with auburn highlights and she was always stylishly attired. Even now, relaxing at home, she was wearing a pair of black slacks with a perfect fit and a silk leopard-print blouse. Everything about her was perfect except for the look on her face, which was dangerously neutral. She tilted her head for the brief kiss Alexis pressed on her cheek.

Crossing the threshold into the land of no return, Alexis took off her coat and followed Aretha, who had Sparkle tucked under her arm, into the dining room. This was where Aretha preferred to stage all interventions and councils of war, as Alexis thought of her mother's lectures. Aretha didn't bother with preliminaries, she just plunged in headfirst.

"Who is this man you're involved with and where did you meet him?"

"Mama, I'm too old for you to be interrogating me like you did when I was a teenager. I have nothing but respect for you, but I'm old enough to handle my own business," Alexis said, politely but firmly. It was the only way to handle Aretha when she was about to go off and Alexis could see that she was itching to do battle.

"I thought you'd put all that foolishness behind you. You don't need a man in your life. It's the last thing you need. You've got your education, you've got your businesses, which are doing extremely well, and you have your own home. What in the world do you need a man for?"

"I take issue with the word *need*. I don't need a man to improve my financial status or offer me security. Suppose I want the company of a man, is that in any way abnormal? I'm not a recluse. I like having a social life and that would include a man. Having a man in my life isn't some kind of dire, aberrant behavior, it's perfectly reasonable.

"What I don't understand is why you think it's so crazy for me to want to date, to mate and act like any other woman?"

Aretha had been playing with Sparkle while Alexis talked. It was another of the weapons in her arsenal of passive-aggressiveness; she would act like she wasn't listening. Now, however, she was ready to speak.

"Alexis, how many times do I have to tell you that this family has a curse on it where men are concerned? My mother, me and my sisters, none of us have had any luck with men. They have lied to us, died on us, mistreated us and cheated on us."

"Mama, that's a total exaggeration. Your grandmother was married until the day she died and you have two sisters who are still quite happily married. Yes, there have been some missteps along the way, but it's not even logical to say there's a curse on the family. As I've told you many, many times over the years, that's just crazy talk."

Aretha gave her a sly look, the look of someone about to play their trump card. "And what about you? Remember that so-called fiancé of yours?"

"Old news, Mama. He was one of those missteps. I'm not the first woman who fell for a man who wasn't fully committed to monogamy. That was a long time ago and I've forgotten it and so should you."

Alexis was tired of the conversation, which they'd had so many times that it was like reading a script. "Look, dear, I'm glad you're back but I've got to run. Maybe next time we can actually discuss the trip instead of my business."

"You think I'm prying when in reality I'm trying to protect you. It just doesn't make sense for an independent woman like you to try and get tied down with a man. You can take care of yourself without all that foolishness."

"Okay, Mama, that's enough for today. When you've calmed down, we'll have a real talk." Alexis got up from her chair and leaned over to kiss her on the cheek. She started walking to the front door with Aretha and Sparkle following.

"By the way, I forgot to tell you thanks for cleaning up the house. I appreciated not coming back to a pigsty."

Alexis smiled over her shoulder. "How did you know it was me?"

"Because I know my children. I knew what this place would look like after Ava was here for a week by herself."

"She's got to grow up sometime, Mama. You're way too easy on her."

"You're right, I know you're right. Something needs to be done about her," Aretha agreed, yet with a shake of her head.

Before Alexis left the porch, Aretha said, "I didn't mean to run you off. I get carried away, I know I do. I just want the very best for you, for all my girls. So is this man good to you?"

"He's very sweet, Mama. His name is Jared and he's a chef and restaurant owner and he's very handsome and kind. Sparkle loved him."

Just then a car pulled up and let out the errant Ava. She joined the two women and before her mother could say anything Ava called out, "Hi, Mama! Did Alexis tell you she's dating a white man?"

Alexis narrowed her eyes at her sister and said two words before she got in her car and drove off.

"You're fired."

Chapter 12

As much as she wanted to, Alexis didn't see Jared the next day. She'd missed him the night before, but they'd been so tired from their respective long days that a good night's sleep sounded like the best plan to both of them. They had talked on the phone for an extended time which was better than nothing, but it certainly wasn't the same as being together. The next day Alexis already had plans to have dinner with Sherri and Sydney and she wasn't the kind of woman to break plans with her girls just to be with a man. Besides, she needed some chat time with Sherri. She found it odd to miss him as much as she did, considering the fact that they'd known each other so briefly, but she felt his absence keenly.

Now they were on their way to Hilton Head for the weekend, albeit a short one. They had decided to drive down Saturday morning and come back on Sunday. In the meantime, they were just going to enjoy each other's company.

Alexis asked, "Have you ever been to Hilton Head before?"

"Lots of times," Jared answered. "My family used to come here a lot in the summer. I've been on my own a few times, too. It's a nice place, very relaxing."

"Even in the winter it's great to visit. It's cool, but you can still walk on the beach."

"Compared to Chicago, it feels like springtime. Do you know how cold it is up there right now?"

Alexis gave a mock shudder and rubbed her hands together as if they were freezing. "No, and I don't want to! I don't do cold weather."

"You get used to it." He reached over and took her hand. "You'd never have to worry about getting cold. I'd find a way to keep you warm."

They exchanged smiles and he placed a kiss on the back of her hand.

"You're very affectionate, aren't you? I'm not complaining, I like it," Alexis assured him. "You're just not shy about showing affection."

Jared didn't say anything for a moment. "Actually, I've never been considered affectionate. It was a major complaint made by most of my previous relationships. I was generally considered to be lacking in spontaneous emotion and conversation."

"You? I find that very hard to believe," Alexis said in surprise.

"It's true, every bit of it. But I find it impossible not to touch you, Alexis. Your skin is so soft and warm, and you smell fantastic. I also enjoy talking to you. I love the way your expressions change when you're saying something interesting. And the sound of your voice drives me crazy. It is almost like you're singing and it makes me want to touch you again."

It was such a sweet declaration that Alexis found herself at a loss for words. Luckily, they had reached Hilton Head and there were other things to deal with, like finding the Realtor and looking at the potential restaurant properties. Jared had a very specific idea of what he needed and he examined the three sites carefully. Two were for lease and one was for sale and he did a lot of calculating to determine which, if any, would make a good location. The Realtor also had several houses available for viewing. The waterfront houses were nice, but not as nice as the one where they would be staying, although Alexis didn't say what she was thinking. There were a couple of fairly mundane ones and another that was quite beautiful, but too small in Jared's opinion.

"Two bedrooms aren't going to be enough," he told Alexis as they drove to Emily's family home. "That's just barely enough room for me, much less a family. I liked it, but it made me a little claustrophobic."

The drive to Emily's home wasn't far from the last house they viewed and they were there in minutes. "Turn left at the intersection and then make a right. The driveway is really long and it curves," she cautioned him.

The first sight of the imposing house was very impressive. Emily's late father had been an architect and a builder and the house was his design. They came through the back door and Alexis disarmed the security keypad. The first room they entered was the big, airy kitchen. Jared gave a low whistle as he looked around the space.

"Very nice," he approved. "This is definitely a cook's kitchen."

"My friend's mom is a wonderful cook and she told her husband exactly what she wanted. Come see the rest of it," she urged, taking his hand and leading into the dining room.

By the time the tour was complete, Jared was totally taken with the house. The interior was open and filled with light from the big windows throughout. The walls were all paneled in oak and the high ceilings had matching beams and black ceiling fans. A big screened porch extended around three sides of the house, offering shade and comfortable lounging in the summer. In the back of the house, accessible by the kitchen entry, was a big deck with an overhang that protected a hot tub. Jared looked down at Alexis and asked if she'd ever used a hot tub in cold weather.

She frowned and said no. "Not in hot weather or cold. Ever since I first heard about MRSA and all those other diseases, a hot tub just looks like a giant bowl teeming with germs. No, thank you. It's drained, anyway. They always drain and cover it for the winter."

He put his arms around her and pulled her in close for a long kiss. "That's kind of sad. I have a long-standing fantasy involving a hot tub and a beautiful woman."

Alexis loved the feel of him against her body. "I have a compromise in mind," she said mischievously. "I happen to know that there's a huge master bathtub. Maybe we can work on a reality that's better than a fantasy."

After more kissing, they went upstairs to see the rest of the house and the bathtub was indeed enormous. Jared was all for trying it out right there and then, but Alexis suggested they wait until the house warmed up. Even though a service came to clean it once a month, they didn't leave the heat on in the cold months so it was decidedly chilly. Jared agreed it could wait until later, although not much later, he emphasized. They went downstairs and he unloaded the car while Alexis started a fire. The day, which had started out bright and sunny, was now completely overcast with a distinct smell of rain.

"Looks like we're getting some rain," she said.

"Is that a good thing or a bad thing?" Jared asked.

"For me it's a very good thing. I love rain. There's nothing nicer than a long rainy afternoon with nothing to do."

"Yes, there is. A long rainy afternoon with someone you adore, someone you desire more than anyone else. That's my idea of a perfect day."

"I stand corrected," Alexis said softly.

They went over to the huge sectional sofa and got comfortable, Jared stretched out to his full length and Alexis lying on top of him, their legs entwined and her head nestled under his chin. He reached for a soft handmade throw and put it over her.

He couldn't ever remember feeling this content. He came to Columbia to open a restaurant and he ended up opening his heart. He wasn't kidding when he'd told Alexis that he'd had a reputation for being elusive and standoffish in matters of the heart. He was a good guy; he'd never deliberately hurt a woman but he couldn't pretend to feel emotions that he didn't have. He had a lot of female friends, he'd had pleasant relationships in the past, but no one had ever made him feel the way Alexis did. His father had always told him and his brothers that when you met the right woman, you'd know. There would be no hesitation, no game-playing; it would be a feeling of certainty like no other. Jared felt the easy, even breathing that meant Alexis was asleep. He kissed the top of her head and enfolded her even closer before he drifted off to join her.

Alexis awoke to the sound of rain. It was pouring, just as she'd predicted. The room was now pleasantly warm and the crackling of the fire was the perfect counterpoint to the weather. Jared's heartbeat was familiar and soothing and she felt perfectly relaxed. The past few days had been absolutely crazy but she couldn't remember being happier or more content. If the recent events had been on paper, she would have scoffed and tossed the book, if that's what it was, in the trash.

I left book club on Monday and had a flat in a storm. A strange man I thought was a vampire rescued me. Then I rescued him, and took him to the emergency room. He tells them I'm his fiancée so I can stay with him. Then he gets loopy on pain meds and kisses me. On Tuesday I go get him to take him to his car and we spend the day together. He comes to pick me up for dinner, he recites a poem by Langston Hughes and I melt like butter. We spend the night doing things I didn't know my body was capable of and he writes me a poem the next morning. He defends my honor on Wednesday and spends the night again. We took Thursday off, I was with Sherri on Friday and here we are Saturday. He's from a different state, a different city and a different race and I feel as if I know him better than anyone I've ever met in my life. This movie would get two thumbs down for being mawkish and unrealistic from any movie critic in America but it feels so real. I've really gone off the deep end.

Her mind was racing but her body was still. She was just too comfortable to move. She was waiting for the weird feeling of anxiety to creep over her, the one that told her with certainty that she'd committed some heinous error of judgment that was going to come back and bite her, but it didn't come. She tried to marshal up reasons why she should run far away from Jared and stay hidden, but she couldn't think of any.

There was Aretha, of course; she was so paranoid about the "family curse" that Alexis could have marched up to her door with Idris Elba on one arm and Delroy Lindo on the other and her mother would still find a reason to go postal. The fact that Jared was white wasn't as problematic as the fact that he was a man. She did, however, make a mental note to get Ava back at her earliest opportunity. The only reason Ava had mentioned Jared's race was to focus Aretha's attention away from her transgressions.

Alexis had to laugh when thinking about the crazy women in her family. They were all lovable in their unique ways and all certifiable. Her soft laughter gently roused Jared. His hands moved around until they were cupping her butt.

"What's so funny?"

"Just thinking about my crazy mother," she said.

"You're supposed to be thinking about me, beauty."

She was about to give him a seductive answer when both of their stomachs started growling in unison. Their eyes met and they burst into laughter.

"I think better on a full stomach, Jared."

"By all means, let me get you fed because I want all of you focused on me. Let's go," he said, gripping her behind as he sat and swung his legs onto the floor. He picked her up and carried her into the kitchen with her legs around her waist, laughing the whole way.

Chapter 13

They had stopped at a grocery store with a good deli section on the way to the house and picked up a variety of food for a picnic-type meal. After sitting by the fire consuming the chicken salad with grapes, mixed green salad, roast beef, artisanal bread and two kinds of cheese, Jared cleaned up everything and put out the fire while Alexis went upstairs to start filling the giant bathtub.

The tub had a lot to offer in terms of its capacity, which was at least three adults, but it took forever to get it filled with hot water. She watched the water level rise at an annoyingly slow rate while she considered what to put in the water. She decided on her bottle of Magno bath gel. It was made in Spain and it had a fresh, clean smell that was suitable for a man or a woman. Satisfied with her choice, she went to the bedroom to get her iPod dock, stopping at the linen closet for more big fluffy towels.

When Jared came up the stairs with a bottle of wine, two

glasses, a bowl of ice and some sliced kiwi and peaches, he was greeted by the sight of Alexis standing next to the tub watching the bubbles rise. A wonderful sound filled the room; it was the voice of Landau Eugene Murphy, Jr. Alexis loved his rich voice and the jazz standards he favored. She was singing along softly, and she was nude except for a tiny pair of panties in red lace that were the most amazing things he'd ever seen. They barely covered anything but the essentials and they came down into a deep vee between her firm brown globes.

"You're trying to give me a heart attack, aren't you?"

She turned around and gave him a cheeky grin and he could see that the same vee was in the front. "Absolutely not. Go take off your clothes, it's full."

He quickly put down the tray in the bedroom they were using and removed his clothes in record time. He returned to the bathroom just as Alexis was shimmying out of the delightful panties.

"What are those things? They're worth whatever you paid for them."

"They're by Hanky Panky, aren't they cute? I have lots of them."

Jared stepped into the tub and held her hands as she followed him. "I'm going to have to get you a supply of those in case I wreck any in a fit of passion," he told her as they sank into the hot, fragrant bubbles. "Damn, this feels good."

"I'm about to make it better," Alexis said. "Turn around and hand me that bath gel."

She wet the brand-new nylon bath puff she'd brought with her and poured a little of the amber gel onto it. Working up a lather, she began to scrub his neck gently in small circles, then his shoulders and his long back. She did his sides and his arms and had him turn around to face her so she could give his front the same treatment. When she finished, it was her turn for him to cover her with foam. Soon every inch of her body was treated to his loving, methodical care. He spent the most time on her breasts, using his hands to slowly circle the sweet mounds until the soothing bath had turned into something totally different.

He lay against the high side of the tub with Alexis on his chest. Her bottom rested against his hardened manhood as his fingers began to explore the treasure between her legs.

"I love your hair," Jared said idly. "It's always so pretty, and you never care if it gets wet."

"That's one of the reasons I keep it short, I swim so much that it would be impractical to have long hair. And I'm not crazy about long hair, either. Women used to wear a hairstyle, now they just want long, long hair hanging down, getting tangled up, weaves and lace-front wigs that make most of them look like horses and give them traction alopecia. It's just not my thing."

"When did you learn how to swim?"

"I was probably three. Daddy's brother drowned when he was a child and he insisted that all of us learn to swim. Apparently, I'm part fish because I really took to it. I teach a swimming class for kids who normally wouldn't learn how. Whenever I read about children drowning at a swim party or at the beach, I just freak out. I even give the girls half-off on a shampoo and set afterward because that's why some children don't learn to swim. Their mamas are afraid it'll wreck their hair. So when did you start swimming?"

"I was two, according to my dad. I was that skinny, geeky kid who was always slightly damp with goggles around his neck, smelling like chlorine because I never stayed away from the water. Total swim team nerd from middle school on. But I got a full scholarship so it paid off."

Alexis laughed at the idea of Jared being skinny and geeky; the image just wouldn't materialize. "I wasn't geeky, but I was skinny. People used to make the mistake of teasing me because I'm dark-skinned and it never worked because my daddy told me I was an ebony princess descended from a long line of African queens. Anytime somebody would try and make me feel bad, I'd just put it down to jealousy and ignorance. Then I'd go win something to piss them off. I was the head cheerleader, homecoming queen, prom queen, captain of the swim team and I was voted most popular girl in senior class. I had a lot of female frenemies, but I had lots of male admirers. My daddy never should have started that princess thing." She giggled. "I believed every word."

Jared agreed with her. "He was right. You are descended from a line of African queens. But you're not a princess anymore, you're a goddess, remember? You have the most amazing skin, Alexis. It's why I can't keep my hands off you. Even when I'm not with you, I have this sense memory that makes me tingle when I think about touching you."

Her eyes opened to see his much lighter hands stroking her dark body and a thought popped into her head. "Jared, am I the first black woman you've ever dated?"

He laughed softly and said no. "Not by any means. I'm an international lover, baby."

She flicked a few drops of water in his face and said, "I don't know about that. I think I'll need a demonstration to evaluate your credentials."

She rose to a standing position and reached for the handheld shower. "The water's getting a little cold. How about I turn up the heat?"

Jared leaned over and pressed the lever drain the tub before standing up to join her. She rinsed all the foam from his body with pulsating jets of water, changing the setting to give his manhood an imaginative and thorough massage. He returned the favor, rinsing her clean before stimulating her already tingling breasts. The pulsing spray concentrated on her nipples wasn't quite like having his talented mouth on them, but the sensation aroused her all the same. So when he used a higher setting between her legs, she had to hold on to his broad shoulders for support as her climax rippled through her in wave after wave of pleasure.

After the water play, they were both ready for much more. They patted each other dry and went to the bedroom where a king-size bed awaited them, but Alexis insisted on laying down two thick bath sheets first. She had Jared sit down on the towels and picked up a bottle of Moroccan oil. He looked mystified until she said, "In about ten minutes I'm going to give you the best massage you've ever had."

"Why the wait?" he asked.

She knelt next to him on the bed, smiling seductively. She stroked his rock-hard erection, moving her hand up and down, her thumb circling the broad circumference of the head, already throbbing and ready. "Because I have something else in mind," she murmured.

When her lips touched him, opening so that her tongue could stroke him, Jared felt a shocking pleasure that shook him to his core. Her soft hand held him firmly, stroking him as she took him in, swirling her tongue around while she cupped and caressed the base. He could feel his control slipping, the sensations were too intense and he wanted to be inside her when he came. When she started flicking her tongue across the tip, teasing every fold and crevice, he had to pull her into his lap, thrusting into her before standing up. Her legs went around him automatically and neither one of them held back.

He started slow, pushing into her firmly but gently until the rhythm was right and then he pumped into her body harder and faster. With nothing between them except skin, he could feel every bit of her, every squeeze of her inner walls and she clamped and held him over and over. Her hands clasped his shoulders and her back arched as she took everything he had, meeting his furious passion with one of her own. Her nipples were huge and hard and her eyes were closed, her long eyelashes fluttering as she moaned his name. His hands gripped her hips and held on tight as they rode out their massive climax together. Her eyes opened and the look she gave Jared pushed him over the brink into another climax. When he finally lowered them to the bed, he couldn't let her go.

He lay down and rolled her over so that Alexis was on her back and he treated each gorged nipple to a long, sucking kiss before licking his way down to her sweetness. Guiding her legs over his shoulders, he kissed her like he was kissing her mouth. He could still feel her throbbing, taste her juicy response to their loving. He used his tongue to savor every bit of her, licking and tonguing and sucking her into climaxing again and again. When he was sure she was satisfied, he gently lowered her legs and changed positions so that she was on his chest, next to his heart.

There wouldn't be any talking or massaging for a while, but the closeness they shared was much more precious.

Much later, after their hearts stopped pounding and they could remember their own names again, Alexis made good on her promise of a massage. Jared insisted on giving her one first, which touched her to no end.

"Ladies are always first, goddess. I've heard my female friends bemoan the fact that whoever gives the first massage gets left out because the recipient goes to sleep. So it's my pleasure to give you pleasure."

He gave a great massage, too. His strokes were firm and sure. He was really good at manipulating every muscle in her body to the point where she felt limp and weightless. The soft scent of the oil and the warmth of his hands were almost too relaxing. When he had her turn over so he could do her front, she was glad because she was about to slip into a deep slumber. He began working on her feet, manipulating each one firmly. He even managed not to tickle her soles, which was heavenly.

"I just realized what sexy feet you have. I noticed that they were pretty and well groomed, but they're extremely sexy."

"My feet?"

"Yes. They're so small and slender, and they're as soft as the rest of you," he said. To prove it, he ran his tongue across her deep rose painted toenails and sucked on her big toe. He licked the bottom of her foot and this time the tickle she'd been dreading came, but it was a different kind of sensation, one that rippled up her body in a shimmering rush. She pulled away her foot and sat up.

"Hey, that's enough of that. For now," she amended. "If you want a rubdown you need to lay back right now or you'll be the one left in the lurch."

He obeyed, although it was difficult. Her chocolate skin gleamed in the candlelight and she looked like something he wanted to eat, every luscious bit of her, but he bowed to her wish and was glad he did. She gave him a tremendous massage, using all of the methods she'd learning in her training, all the methods employed at her spas. She was working her way down his strong legs when she commented that he didn't have any tattoos.

"I'm not complaining because I'm not crazy about them," she said. "It's just that everybody seems to have them these days."

"I have one," Jared admitted. "I got it a long time ago but I had it put somewhere discreet. I didn't want to have to explain it."

Surprised, Alexis asked where it was.

"Look on the inside of my right foot," he answered.

Just as he said, there was a small tattoo. In a small print there were the Olympic rings and the words *Poetry Man*.

Alexis's mouth dropped open and she almost fell off the bed from the sheer shock of seeing it. Maybe he really was hers, after all.

Chapter 14

The next morning Alexis was still rather gobsmacked by the discovery of Jared's tattoo. His explanation for it was simple and unique at the same time, but it didn't lessen the impact of seeing those particular words on his foot.

"I never told you this, but I was in the Olympics my freshman year of college," he said slowly. He sounded a bit self-conscious, which she found endearing. "I competed in 1996 in Atlanta. The team all had nicknames and mine was Poetry Man because, you know, I wrote poetry. And the name Aqua Man was already taken, dammit. So we got tattoos and that's mine."

"You were in the Olympics," she marveled. "That's amazing! I'm an Olympics junkie. I watch, like, every single event but I'm really hooked on track and field and, of course, swimming. Did you win a medal?"

Sounding even more self-conscious, he admitted winning two individual gold medals and a team silver in the relay. Her admiration of his achievement and his modesty grew as he told the story.

"I watched every minute of the '96 Olympics, but I can't remember seeing you. I was really watching the track events because I had a huge crush on Michael Johnson, but I watched all the televised swim events, too."

To her surprise, Jared laughed out loud. "I hope to God you don't remember me because I had shaved every hair off my body including my head and my eyebrows. I looked extra-goofy, especially with the flag decal on the back of my head."

Alexis joined in the laughter, trying to picture him handsome but hairless. "Why in the world did you do that?"

"I lost a bet with my demented brothers. When you meet them, don't mention it because they'll lie and embellish the story for their own twisted amusement," he warned.

The laughter dissolved into kissing and caressing and the whole thing was forgotten except for the oddness of him having those special words permanently etched on his body. Sherri would say that it was a sign, that he was definitely her man. It was true; the secret desire of her heart was to have a man sensitive enough to love poetry and she'd found him. He had every single attribute on her list—well, but that one—and so many more that it was like an embarrassment of riches. But that wealth of charms fell under the heading "too good to be true," didn't it? That's not how real life worked.

Much later they decided to take a long walk on the beach, which suited Alexis just fine. It was cool and windy and the sand was damp, but they wore sneakers and thick socks, jeans and heavy sweaters and Jared kept his arm around her to make good on his promise to always keep her warm. She was wearing her favorite sweater—a thick, wool, cream-colored cable-knit Donna Karan for Men sweater that came down to her knees and had a hood, which she'd pulled snugly over her head. She'd found the sweater on sale in the men's department at T.J. Maxx and it was one of her favorite things to wear in the winter. She usually rolled up the overlong sleeves, but today she left them down so they covered her hands.

They walked and talked and watched the water and the contentment that she always felt when she was with him covered her like a warm blanket. He'd brought the rest of the bread from dinner to feed the seagulls, something she discouraged.

"I'm not too fond of those critters. They've dumped on my car one too many times. They're carp with wings, if you ask me."

When the cloud of noisy gulls descended on the beach to partake of Jared's offering, it became apparent that they weren't alone on the beach. Three small, sturdy dogs came running toward them, barking like mad. Alexis was delighted with them and made friends immediately. Their owners, a young married couple, ran after them and they chatted and introduced the dogs, which were Welsh Corgis, to Alexis. Their names were Astrid, Olivia and Peter, after the main characters in *Fringe,* which Alexis thought was just adorable. They were playful and bright-eyed and her heart was won forever. She kept talking about the dogs as she and Jared walked back to the house.

"Those little faces were so cute! Those big eyes, they're so sweet," she said with a sigh.

Jared grinned down at her. "And ears like satellite dishes," he teased. "You could probably get a hundred stations with those things."

She nudged him in his ribs. "Don't be mean, Jared. Those dogs are the most adorable things ever and you know it."

"I thought you were into Yorkies," he said mildly.

She shook her head. "I love Sparkle but she's a little too delicate for me. She can't jump off the sofa or she'll break one of her tiny legs. I need something sturdy that can really play."

They reached the house and she went to check on the laundry. Alexis had cleaned the kitchen, bedroom and bath. Plus she'd laundered every bit of linen they'd used. She could stay at Emily's family home whenever she wanted, but she took her responsibility as a guest quite seriously. Everything went back into its appointed place, was spotless and secured before she left, as she ensured on every visit. While she finished folding towels, Jared was looking more closely at the pictures on the walls.

"Hey, I know her," he said suddenly.

"Know who?"

"The woman in this picture," he replied, pointing at Emily. "I met her on a plane when I was flying to Chicago last year. She was really nice and we had lunch at VanBuren's. This is your BFF that you talk about all the time?"

Alexis nodded her head, totally bemused. "You're the hunk," she said.

"I'm what?"

"Emily told us she'd met a hunk on the plane and she went out with him. You're the guy that made Todd so jealous," she laughed. "What a crazy coincidence."

"Not coincidence, remember? This is fate. Emily was really nice and very good-looking but if you'd been with her, I wouldn't have paid her much attention. I called her once after Thanksgiving and she told me she'd gotten married and I was happy for her. If you'd told me the same thing, I wouldn't have been happy in the least. That's why you're my fiancée now. I was waiting for you to come into my life."

He grabbed her and planted a big kiss on her eager lips. "Jared, you'd better quit saying that or I'm going to take it seriously one day and then you'll have to explain me to your parents," she warned.

He just laughed and kissed her again, longer and harder.

* * *

The trip to Hilton Head was the end of their first week together and it was like the rich, creamy foam on a cappuccino; the perfect topping to a satisfying treat. But now that they were entering week two, Alexis had no idea what to expect. She wanted to just keep floating along in the rosy bubble they created whenever they were together, but how realistic was that? Was any of it real or was it an extreme case of wishful thinking on her part? Alexis had a habit of overthinking when she was evaluating something really important and this was no exception. She went to the gym at six on Monday morning, plunging into the water and doing laps as though her life depended on it.

Instead of tiring her out, it energized her and she left the gym full of purpose. She had to go to both spas today, but she headed for Sanctuary One first. She had an appointment with Javier for a trim and she had some important news for him, too. They were alone in the salon when she went to his station and sat in his styling chair. She'd already taken off her top and put on the smock they gave clients to wear and Javier draped her with a cape before examining her hair.

"What are we doing today?" he asked.

"Whatever you think it needs, Javier. Definitely a trim and I think it's a little dry," she replied.

"I think a mineral treatment for chlorine buildup and a deep conditioner," he said, rubbing the thick strands between his fingers. "And a caramel gloss to add some shine. All that swimming is hard on your hair, Alexis."

"I know, that's why I condition every day and use a leave-in overnight." Thinking about last week when she certainly had not left conditioner in her hair on several occasions, she amended her answer. "Most of the time," she muttered.

Javier, bless his heart, knew exactly what she meant but he didn't pry. His attention was totally focused on giving her the precise attention she was accustomed to getting from him. Alexis liked her hair short and carefree, but it required an excellent cut to keep it looking fabulous and she preferred Javier's skills above anyone else's. He always trimmed her thick hair dry because it rendered the best results. Once he was finished, he brushed away all the clippings as he removed the cutting cape, replacing it with a shampoo cape. As they went to the shampoo bowl, Alexis asked him a question.

"Javier, what are your career plans for the future? Have you mapped out a five-year plan?"

Javier adjusted the headrest as Alexis leaned back into the bowl. "I've thought about it a great deal, Alexis, as you probably already know. Of course, I'm looking to the future to increase my earnings, to do more in the business, including teaching and eventually owning my own salon and school," he said.

"I appreciate your honesty, Javier. I like the fact that you always give me a straight answer to any question. You're the best stylist I have at either location and you're a team leader. You have a good management style and I don't want to lose you. I've been thinking for some time that I need a manager and I want that person to be you."

Javier looked intrigued. "You want me to manage the salon?"

"No, I want you to manage the whole operation. I want to have an operations manager at both locations and I think you'd be perfect for the position. It would give you a substantial raise, for one thing, and it would be a challenge. What are your thoughts?"

Javier was massaging her scalp with fragrant shampoo while she talked. She was glad they were alone because the sides of the shampoo bowl made her words echo.

"I'm very honored that you're offering me the position,

Alexis. I'd love to take it on, but there are some areas on the administrative side where I'm going to need some training."

"Absolutely, Javier. I'm not going to throw you out there without instruction. Also, I like the idea of a school," she told him. "There're some very good ones out there and then some of them are chop shops, as we both know. That might be an excellent direction for Sanctuary to go in. Have you ever thought about eventually becoming my partner? I have a feeling we could go very far together," she said thoughtfully.

Javier was smiling when she sat up and he deftly put a towel around her head. "Alexis, I've wanted to have this discussion with you for a while. You're talking about something that's been on my mind for a long time."

He applied the deep conditioner and a plastic cap before putting her under the dryer. She looked at her reflection in the mirror and made a face. "Beauty has no pain and no shame. If Jared could see me now," she murmured.

"If he could see you now, all he'd see is your natural beauty. That man has it bad for you, Alexis."

He dropped the hood on the dryer and the noise drowned out anything she might have said. As it was, she was speechless, a rare state for her.

This wasn't a book club night and Jared was busy at the restaurant; he'd warned her he was going to have a late night because he needed to ramp up the progress of the contractors. Plus, the long overdue dining room furniture had arrived but it couldn't be set up without assembly. He figured he'd be working past midnight. Feeling a bit at loose ends, she decided to call Alana and see if she was free for dinner. She was, and they made a date to meet at their favorite rib joint, a place called Sweet Tea & Three Sides. They greeted each other with a big hug and kiss on the cheek.

"You look good, little sister," Alana said approvingly. "It

looks like Javier put the moves on your hair and Jared took care of everything else," she teased.

Alexis ran her hand through her hair which was looking very Halle Berry at the moment. She was dressed casually in a pair of jeans and a violet turtleneck, but her casual was like everybody else's Sunday best. It was all in the details, like her gleaming black riding boots and her giant silver hoop earrings. She smiled wanly when Alana mentioned Jared, but she didn't make a direct response. Instead, she returned the compliment to Alana.

"You're looking fab, too. I must say, you're the most stylish car specialist in the south."

Alana was equally casual in her attire, and equally attractive. Anyone could tell they were sisters from a mile away. And Alana could tell that something was on her little sister's mind.

While they waited for their orders to be served, they both crossed their arms and leaned in a little. Alana, ever forthright, went first.

"Okay, let's get it out on the table. What's up with that blue-eyed passion pole? Are you still seeing him?"

"I saw him every day last week except Thursday, because we were exhausted and Friday because it was dinner with Sherri and Sydney. We went to Hilton Head on Saturday and came back on Sunday," Alexis reported.

"And? You like him? Because he likes you, I could tell even though he was a little bit goofy from the meds. There was definitely something there," Alana said encouragingly.

"Yes, but what's 'something'? Is it a pastime? A fling? A social experiment gone wild, what?"

Alana raised a brow slightly. "What do you want it to be?"

The server came over with their plates of barbecue; rib tips for Alexis and bones for Alana, plus greens, macaroni and cheese, coleslaw and hot corn bread. She placed their glasses of sweet tea on the table and asked if there was anything else.

They told her no and said grace. While Alana tucked into her food with good appetite, Alexis took small bites of her side dishes and pondered what her sister had asked her.

"I'm not completely sure what I want it to be. I know what it feels like when we're together, but what will it be like outside the fantasy land? For instance, he's very close to his family. Can you picture my little black face at their Thanksgiving dinner table? What would his parents do if he brought home a black woman? I'm not talking about a Paula Patton–looking woman. I'm talking about a woman like me. He's dated black women before, but what does that really mean? It doesn't mean he took them home to mom and dad."

Alana daintily wiped her mouth and took a sip of tea before answering. "Let's not worry about his people right now. How would he fit in with *your* people? Not just family, your friends, too. Would he be comfortable sitting down in here or would he be looking over his shoulder every ten seconds thinking he was gonna get shot? What about things like your birthday party, for example? I've noticed that my white friends are willing to go anywhere with me as long as it's on their turf. They'll drag me anywhere without a thought for me being the only speck of pepper in a big bowl of grits. But let me suggest going to the jazz club or anything that's outside of their comfort zone and they start looking crazy."

Alexis finally found her appetite and attacked the rib tips. She had to stop herself from licking the tangy sauce off her fingers, it was so good.

Alana confided that she'd never really wanted to have a serious involvement with someone who wasn't black. "I can't see myself trying to explain what collard greens are, and why I wrap my hair in a scarf at night or any of that good stuff. I really crave familiarity, I guess. I like the idea that the person I'm with has shared experiences and lifestyles. It makes me comfortable."

Alexis felt that familiar hot flush along her cheekbones. "I should have been thinking with my brain instead of letting Miss Alexis do the thinking for me," she said.

They both laughed heartily; it was an old joke between the sisters, they all referred to their lady parts as Miss Alexis, Miss Alana and so on.

"It's really not funny, Alana. I did the deed the day after I met the man! He recited 'When Sue Wears Red' after I opened the door in my red wrap dress and my clothes started flying all over the room. I've never been loose, you know that. But there was just something about him that made Miss Alexis lose her mind."

Alana waved her hand to brush away her sister's angst. "Listen, girl, when it's good and it's right, you know. You just know. I slept with Sam the day we met. I didn't even have a twenty-four-hour waiting period, so I can't talk. And he was the love of my life, and I was his," she said sadly.

Sam was her college sweetheart who had tragically died five years after they married and Alana had never gotten over it. Alexis reached over and patted her hand. There wasn't much she could say after that. Alana was not at a loss for words, though.

"Look, this is what you need to do. Break out of the bubble. Start seeing him in different surroundings, expose him to different situations and see how he does. Then you'll know."

"You make it sound like I'm giving him a test, or a series of tests. Like I'm putting him on double secret probation or something."

Alana grinned and shrugged. "It's just a suggestion. But it's a way of getting to the heart of the matter. You obviously like this guy and he likes you. If you want it to be more than a fling and whatever, you need to know some things. I'm just sayin'."

Alexis mulled it over for a while as she savored the last of her greens. Then something occurred to her. "By the way, thanks for spilling the beans to Mama. That just made my day. Heifer."

Alana burst out laughing. "I'm sorry, but she was getting in my business so I had to shift her attention. I owe you one, I really do."

"Yes, well, our darling little sister was doing the same thing. I was leaving the house, almost to the car, almost to freedom, mind you, and little Ava comes home and sees that look in Mama's eyes so she throws me right under the bus. 'Hi, Mama! Did Alexis tell you she's dating a white man?'"

"No, that little wench didn't!"

"Yes, she did. I told her she was fired but I didn't mean it. But isn't it time she went back to school? She only has one semester left."

"That's her problem. Your problem is the blue-eyed passion pole. Deal with him."

In her own big-sister way, Alana was absolutely right.

Chapter 15

The next day Alexis didn't give too much more thought to her conversation with Alana. She was busy all day. Swimming at the gym, Chamber of Commerce meeting, morning at Sanctuary One, Women's Business League luncheon, Sanctuary Two in the afternoon; she was good and tired by the time she finally called it a day. She was the last one to leave Sanctuary Two and she'd just set the alarm and locked up when her cell phone rang. She smiled widely because she knew it was Jared when Phoebe Snow started singing. She'd programmed the phone to play what else but "Poetry Man" when he called her number.

"Hello, beauty. I hope your day was better than mine," he said wearily.

He sounded so tired that Alexis's heart melted. While they talked, Alexis had an inspiration. "Why don't you take a nice hot shower and relax," she suggested.

"Will you come over?"

"I might," she teased.

"If you don't, I'll come find you," he warned her.

"Go take a shower and I'll see you later."

When they ended the call, Alexis went home and took a quick shower of her own, changing out of her fashionable daytime attire into her most bootylicious jeans, her riding boots, a chartreuse tank top and a fuchsia chunky-knit cardigan that stopped right above her waist. She didn't reapply her full makeup; she just added mascara, a hint of blush and a Juicy lip gloss. Before leaving the house, she applied a little perfume and called in an order to her favorite Thai restaurant. She arrived at Jared's loft about an hour after she talked to him.

He opened the door wearing very old jeans and an equally old cardigan sweater. His hair was still damp from the shower and he looked sleepy and sexy. His eyes widened once he saw Alexis.

"Come in, Alexis. You brought me dinner? You're a wonderful woman," he said fervently.

"I hope you like Thai food," she said. "I should have asked, but it would have spoiled the surprise."

"I love it," he said. "Although to be honest, I'm so hungry that I'd happily eat Kibbles 'n Bits right about now. You're a beautiful, thoughtful, special woman." His words of praise were followed by a deep, long kiss.

Jared put out plates, bowls and napkins on the kitchen bar, as well as big tumblers that he filled with ice and sweet green tea. Alexis took out the containers and the chopsticks and served the aromatic dishes.

"What would I do without you, beauty? You know, it occurs to me that one of these days we're going to have to eat a meal at a real table."

"I'll hold you to that. I know exactly what I want, too."

"Whatever you want, it's yours."

Once he sat down on the stool next to hers and started eating, Alexis asked him about his day. He smiled wryly and swallowed a mouthful of pad thai before answering.

"My day was what is often referred to as a key learning experience. I had a moment of clarity that told me I'm doing too much and I'm getting in my own way. It's kind of ridiculous for me to be doing so much hands-on stuff. I have a tendency to try to control everything and I'm killing myself. Therefore, I'm going to get my brothers and Roland more involved in this enterprise. They're my partners and I should spread the joy. If I don't stop overextending myself, I'm going to burn out. And that was my day. An epiphany."

Alexis reached over and rubbed the back of his free hand. "It's odd that you had that kind of day. I've been warned over and over that I'm also on the verge of burnout and I've actually been giving it a lot of thought. And I took a positive step forward. I promoted my top stylist to spa manager and we're seriously negotiating a partnership. I've finally realized that I have to be in charge, but I don't have to do everything by myself."

Jared leaned over to kiss her cheek. "Brilliant. It's funny how we're in sync on our business matters."

Alexis smiled. "Another coincidence," she said teasingly.

"Not a coincidence. We are simply two overworked people who've decided to take a much-deserved break and it couldn't have come at a better time," he countered. "I need to be able to spend more time with you and I can't do it if I'm trying to be the HMFIC 24/7," he said as he cupped her face with one hand and stared deeply into her eyes. The tender expression made her heart turn to mush as he continued to explain.

"I'm sending for my posse. This is the last time I try to be my own project manager. Incredibly ambitious and stupid at the same time. By the way, did I tell you I have to go to New York?"

"Yes, you did mention it, but you didn't say when you were going."

"I need to go up tomorrow but I'll be back on Friday. I have to tape a show at Food Network and interview some potential sous chefs. I'll be getting Lucas and Damon to handle the rest of the line cooks and my HR manager to handle the waitstaff. I have no flaming idea why I thought I could do this one on my own but guess what? I won't do it again, trust."

"So you're going to be gone for a couple days? Have you made reservations? Packed?"

"Yes and no. I've made reservations but I haven't packed anything. Packing is one of my least favorite things to do. It's a satanic ritual as far as I'm concerned."

Alexis laughed at his foolishness and told him she might be persuaded to help him. "I happen to enjoy the task and I do it very well. So if you're really, really nice to me, I could do you that little favor." She made a squeaking sound of surprise when Jared reached over and pulled her off her stool onto his lap.

"I'll do anything you want for as long as you want me to do it, how's that?"

"Great. Come to church with me on Sunday."

Jared's eyebrows went up and he said, "I'd planned on doing something much more carnal, but sure, I'd like that. Now let's go get my bag before you change your mind."

They did manage to make time for quite a few very carnal things before Jared left Wednesday morning. Alexis had offered to take him to the airport, but he refused.

"I know how busy you are. I can handle it. I'll just miss you that much more," he said before cupping her face in his hands and giving her a truly spectacular goodbye kiss.

He really had a way of making her feel special. Even though she was already missing him, she was in a good mood on Tuesday morning. She had a new client at Sanctuary One and she looked forward to meeting her. She was in the office checking the supply order when Ava came back to let her know that her client had arrived.

Alexis noticed her sister's melancholy expression and asked what was wrong. Ava gave a deep, dramatic sigh before answering.

"Lexie, can I please come live with you for a while? Mama is on my case 24/7 and it's making me neurotic."

"No, you may absolutely not come and stay with me. Try picking up after yourself once in a while, that'll calm her down somewhat. But, chick, you're on your own. Big sister is not offering you shelter."

Her customer was Mrs. Vanessa Lomax, Lucie Porter's friend from Chicago. She was visiting the area and was actually on her way to Hilton Head but she wanted a haircut.

"Mrs. Lomax, it will be an absolute pleasure to style your hair. It's gorgeous and so are you," Alexis said warmly.

She was a lovely lady in her late fifties or early sixties, but her smooth cocoa-colored skin could have belonged to a woman two decades younger. The only thing that gave her away was her white hair that shimmered like platinum. She was small and trim and wore her hair in a short, chic style.

They hit it off at once and chatted away while Alexis shaped her hair, shampooed and conditioned it and gave her a rinse to make the strands sparkle.

"How long are you going to be in Columbia?"

"I'm only here for the day, and then I'm off to attend a conference on Hilton Head."

"Really? Hilton Head is beautiful year-round, but it's nicer in the warm weather. You should come back then," Alexis told her.

"I do plan to," Mrs. Lomax assured her. "My husband and I are retiring down here next year."

"How nice for you. I have to say, though, you look a long way from retirement age."

Mrs. Lomax's eyes twinkled with amusement. "Thank you so much. You're such a sweet young woman. Lucie spoke so highly of you and I can see why. If I could, I'd introduce you to my son. I'm trying to get him married," she added in a conspiratorial whisper. "I think you and D.J. would hit it off. But I'm sure some lucky man has already claimed you as his own."

Alexis's faced was transformed by a beautiful smile. "Yes, he has."

"I knew it," Mrs. Lomax said with clear regret in her voice. "I keep telling him to get a move on or all the best ones will be taken."

After Mrs. Lomax left the salon, Alexis thought about what the older woman had said as she meticulously restored her styling area to its usual pristine condition. She was taken, but for how long? Was she a permanent investment for Jared, or a payday advance loan? And did she have any right to ask since they hadn't discussed any kind of long-term anything?

Here I go again. My mind is spinning in circles and I'm analyzing every word, every gesture, every everything. I'm getting to be as neurotic as Ava.

She looked at the clock on the wall and realized that she had the luxury of some free time. She decided to take a yoga class to relax and get centered. If she couldn't use the superb services at her own spa, who could? Some quality time in the incense-scented studio with the quiet music and guided contemplation would settle her mind. And if it didn't, there was always a nice glass of wine.

Chapter 16

Alexis found that missing Jared was both unexpected and oddly pleasant. He'd only been gone for two days and she already felt as if she'd lost something precious, something of great sentimental value that simply couldn't be replaced. At the same time, she was tingling with the anticipation of seeing him again. It was like waiting for Christmas to come, knowing that she would get a wonderful gift. She hadn't had this kind of goofy, giddy feeling in so long that she didn't recognize it at first; then she realized that she was just feeling like any other woman in the first throes of romance. The fact that he called her several times after he got to New York only emphasized the feeling. She loved hearing his sexy voice; the sound of it made her miss him even more. She was about to blurt out those very words but Jared spoke first.

"Alexis, I can't believe how much I miss you. We've only been apart for a couple of days and I feel like I'm missing a limb or something. I believe you put a spell on me," he said. "By the way, you left something at the loft."

"I did? What was it?"

"Your gold bracelets. I forgot to tell you the morning I left. I put them on top of the small chest next to the bed."

Alexis automatically grasped her left wrist where the bracelets normally were and sure enough, they were missing. "Jared, I think you did something to me, not the other way around. Those are my favorite things and I've never, ever left them anywhere. I'm so glad you found them."

"If you want to get them now, you can. I put one of my keys on your key ring," he told her. "Or you can wait until I come back, which might be sooner than I planned."

"You gave me your key? Wow, that's deep," Alexis said with a smile. "The key exchange is supposed to be the turning point in a relationship. I know people who've broken up over the key thing."

Jared laughed and the deep sound of his voice sent a thrill racing through her body. "That has nothing to do with us, beauty. We're on a totally different level from the rest of the world. If you decide to get the bracelets before I get back, just use your key and go on in."

They ended the conversation too soon, but they both had a long day ahead of them. Alexis had three appointments at Sanctuary One, a staff meeting at Sanctuary Two plus a few interviews. She thrived on all the activity, but the absence of her bracelets was distracting. Over the years she'd developed a habit of shaking the bracelets down and fingering them while she was deep in thought. As the day wore on she noticed how often she made the gesture and how crazy it looked to be shaking her arm with nothing on it. On the way home at last, she decided to stop at Jared's loft and retrieve her bracelets. Just the thought of having her bangles back made her happy and she was singing a little tune as she pulled into a parking space in front of the building.

After using Jared's key, she turned the old brass handle on the big mahogany door and was about to enter when the door swung wide open from the inside.

"Surprise!"

Alexis's jaw tightened and her eyes narrowed as she faced a tall, bosomy blonde wearing only a towel and damp hair. "And just who the hell are you?"

The woman's eyes widened and she made the mistake of smirking at Alexis. "I'm Kellie. Jared's not here right now, did you want to leave a message for him?"

"I'm about to give you a message you don't want to hear, so I'd suggest you put on some clothes if you don't want to get tossed out of here naked." Alexis was holding on to her temper by a very slender thread.

She punched Jared's auto-dial number on her cell phone so hard she almost dropped it while *Kellie* decided to heed the message that Alexis was giving her loud and clear. She disappeared into the bedroom and while Alexis was leaving a message for Jared on his cell, the woman returned wearing skinny jeans and buttoning a blouse.

"Look, obviously Jared didn't tell you about me," she started in a rather nonchalant tone for a woman who was about to lose a handful of hair if Alexis didn't calm down.

"What was Jared supposed to tell me about you?" Alexis was surprised she could get the words out because her throat was clogged with pure rage.

"Kellie" tried the smirk again and saw at once that this wasn't a smiley situation. She dropped the phony grin and cleared her throat. "I'm here to help Jared set up his new restaurant, and I, um, well…" Her voice faded away as Alexis took a step toward her.

"What are you doing with my bracelets on?" Her voice was low and deadly and she was in no mood to repeat herself.

"They were, umm, on the nightstand and I…"

Alexis felt as though there were flames shooting out of her ears. "You just thought you'd help yourself? Take them off *now*."

"There's no reason to get an attitude." Kellie sniffed. "Just calm down," she added as she struggled to get the slender bangles over her rather meaty hands.

Kellie had no way of knowing that she'd just put both her big flat feet on the green mile. There were few things that could make her angrier than being told to calm down or that she had an attitude. Whoever thought that telling someone to calm down was a way of making them become relaxed and compliant was a total fool. Alexis could feel her blood pressure rising and her fingers flexing around the strap of her purse. She was filled with a primitive rage that made her want to turn the cocky wench upside down and use her scraggly extensions as a mop. She stood perfectly still, though, and waited for the woman to return the bracelets. It gave Alexis a lot of pleasure to see that her hand was shaking as she did.

"There you go. Although I'm just taking your word for it that they belong to you," she said in a snotty voice.

That did it for Alexis. She slipped her bracelets back on her wrist where they belonged and wrapped the strap of her Prada bag around her hand. It looked like a weapon but the real purpose was to keep her from bashing the cow right in her head. "Trust me, they're mine. And even if they weren't, you've got one hell of a lot of nerve to take something that belongs to someone else. That's the sign of a truly common woman."

"Like taking someone else's man?"

The heat of utter fury was burning Alexis from head to toe. If she didn't get away from this Kellie person, the skanky bitch would be taking her teeth home in a bag. And for all she knew, she could very well be poaching on Kellie's territory. She barely knew Jared and he'd never mentioned having a girlfriend or fiancée or wife or whatever this heifer was. Suddenly the rage turned to sheer exhaustion and all Alexis wanted was to get the hell out of the loft and go home. She kept her grip on the purse because she loved her Prada bag and she didn't want to risk ruining the purse by bashing Kellie in the head. Alexis was tired of the whole ugly scene. Without another word she turned and left the loft. She was so steamed up, she didn't take the elevator down, she stomped down the stairs. When the cold air hit her as she exited the building, she took a few deep breaths as she beat a hasty retreat to her car. She hadn't been this angry and hurt since she discovered her fiancé in bed with his ex-girlfriend. That miserable business had made her swear off men and now she was feeling the same way. *Soul mate my behind,* she thought angrily. *I must have "Boo-Boo the fool" tattooed across my forehead.* She was so wrought up that she didn't see Jared's Rover pulling up as she made her escape.

Jared hit the horn as he realized that Alexis was leaving. He'd come home early because he just couldn't stand to be away from her for another minute. As soon as the show finished taping he began his preparations for leaving New York. He'd planned to leave the next day but he wanted to be back in Columbia with Alexis more than he wanted to hang out with his crew in New York. He decided to unload the car and call her when he got upstairs; it wasn't that late and he was sure she would want to get together as soon as possible.

When he reached the loft, he was surprised to hear a woman's voice. He opened the door and his face contorted into a look of astonishment combined with displeasure when he saw Kellie sitting on his couch talking on her cell phone.

"What the hell are you doing in my house?" There was no warmth in his tone because he was anything but glad to see her. Kellie was an executive sous chef at one of his Chicago restaurants and this was the last place he wanted or expected to see her. She had made it plain that she was more than interested in him and he thought he'd made it clear that he didn't want anything to do with her outside the restaurant. She was cocky enough to think that she could win him over and this was her most outrageous attempt to date.

"Listen, I'll call you back. Jared just got home," she said in a breathy voice as she ended the call.

"Jared, I wasn't expecting you so soon," she purred, standing up and thrusting out her sizeable chest like an invitation.

"I wasn't expecting you at all. What the hell are you doing here?"

Kellie finally registered the fact that Jared was upset with her and she started stammering out an explanation. "Damon said you needed help with the new restaurant and since Lucas and Roland went to New York to do *Iron Chef* with you, that only left him. But his kids got sick and I volunteered to come in his place."

"You still haven't explained how you came to be in my home without an invitation," Jared said in an icy voice, crossing his arms over his broad chest and staring at her with little liking.

"Well, Damon gave me your key to the restaurant and your house key was on the same ring," she mumbled. "I wanted to surprise you. I was going to cook you dinner and since we've never had a chance to get together in Chicago, I thought this was the perfect place and time for a rendezvous." She tossed her still-damp hair over her shoulder and gave him her best approximation of a smoldering look.

"Are you out of your mind? I've made it quite plain that I'm not interested in you, Kellie. I don't date employees, for one thing and for another, you're not my type. You've showed an amazing lack of good judgment in this situation. How dare you invade my privacy? Are you that desperate or are you just real crazy and I never noticed?"

Kellie's face turned a mottled, unbecoming red and it was her turn to cross her arms. "I'm not your type? I'm everybody's type, I'll have you know. I get hit on every day of the week," she said angrily.

"You should've accepted an offer, in that case. How long have you been here and how long will it take you to get out?"

"I've been here since this morning. So who is your type, that pint-size hoochie with the bad attitude?"

Jared's face flushed with heat and he turned a bright maroon from sheer rage. "You really are out of your mind. Your bra size is probably bigger than your IQ. You have thirty minutes to get you and your things out of here and I will expect your resignation letter on my desk by tomorrow."

Her pale blue eyes got huge and welled up with tears. "Where am I supposed to go? How am I supposed to get a flight out of here on such short notice? I dropped everything to come down and help you out and this is the way you treat me?"

Her voice turned from what she thought was sultry to a really annoying whine and Jared wasn't moved in the least. On the contrary, he was getting madder by the minute. "The kind of help you came to give me I don't require, not now, not ever. If you were a man, you'd have a split lip right about now because no one talks about my woman the way you just did and gets away with it. The only hoochie in my home today was you and you now have twenty-seven minutes to clear out of here. As far as where you're supposed to go, I don't know and I don't care but you have to get the hell up outta here."

He grabbed his cell, fumbled through his phone book and

punched a button. "Time for a rain check?" A short silence was ended with "now."

He gave her a look of disdain, shaking his head as he continued to speak. "You know, you had a real opportunity with my company and you could have greatly improved your résumé and learned a lot, but instead, you chose to act like the worst kind of bimbo and you blew it. In case you haven't noticed, good opportunities for women are hard to come by in the culinary world. I know how tough it is for women chefs to get the breaks they deserve and I'm really disappointed that you didn't take your position more seriously."

As the finality of his words fully sank in, Kellie went from whiny to weepy. "I do take my job seriously! All I've ever wanted to do was be a world-class chef and I can do it," she protested.

"Good luck with that," Jared said dryly. "I suggest that you keep your activities confined to the kitchen from now on and never, ever try to seduce a man who's let you know he's not interested, especially when he's the one who signs your paycheck."

She sniffed loudly and used her sleeve to wipe her leaking eyes and nose. "Am I really fired?"

"Of course you are. You invaded my privacy and I have no doubt that you insulted my woman. You're lucky I don't press charges against you. You have twenty-two minutes to clear out of here before I change my mind about calling the police," he said in an even tone that left no mistake about his sincerity. "I suggest we put an end to this sordid conversation and you get to stepping. I have plans for the evening that do not include you."

Kellie swept out of the living room and into the kitchen dragging the shreds of her dignity behind her while Jared ground his teeth together so hard he risked breaking them.

Something told him that his reunion with Alexis wasn't going to go the way he'd planned.

A knock at the door gave him some solace.

Alexis left the loft intending to go home, but she found herself driving around aimlessly. Her mind was racing and her temper was still at a high boil. She started in the direction of Alana's house but she changed her mind and headed for Sherri's condo. Halfway there she decided that she wasn't really ready to sit down and have a long sisterly talk with anybody. She tightened her grip of death on the steering wheel and drove home. She was going to turn off the phone, take a hot shower and have a glass of wine or two. Or five.

After reaching the sanctuary of her cozy home, Alexis wasted no time in getting out of her clothes and into a hot shower. She lathered up with Chanel No. 5 bath gel, something she saved for those times when she really wanted to pamper herself and this was one of those times. Every inch of her body was treated to an overly brisk scrubbing with her lavender bath puff while she tried to put her thoughts together. She was mad as hell and her feelings were hurt by the sordid little scene in the loft and she needed to get her mind right before Jared came back to Columbia. If he returned ever; for all she knew, this could be his sneaky, cowardly way of dumping her. They were virtual strangers. This could be his modus operandi for relationships; come to town, fall into bed with the first warm and willing body he could find and then ditch her as fast as possible.

When Alexis finally got out of the shower, her skin was tingling and her scalp was tender from the merciless scrubbing she'd given herself. She'd taken the concept of washing that man right out of her hair to the extreme with punishing thoroughness. Feeling like the world's biggest fool, she wrapped her now-sore head in a towel and slathered Chanel

No. 5 body cream and lotion all over her body before putting on her favorite pajamas. They were cut like men's pj's and a little too big, but the fact that they were silk and a beautiful shade of pink made them feminine and cute. After patting the excess water out of her hair, she applied Moroccan oil and let it air dry into a mass of tight ringlets.

If this Kellie wench was really Jared's woman, Alexis knew she'd made a horrible mistake. If he preferred a tall bleached blonde with big jiggly tits, he should've stayed in that lane instead of crossing over to hers. Alexis had to face the fact that it was Kellie's ethnicity or lack thereof that was at the root of her anger and pain. She tidied up the bedroom before going to the kitchen to pour herself a big glass of wine. It was a cheap Moscato that she liked and it was icy cold, which was how she preferred her wine. A big, unladylike swallow was just what she needed and she followed it with two more. If she was going to be miserable all night, there was no reason that she needed to be sober.

Taking the glass of wine and the bottle into the living room, she turned on the gas fire and plopped her iPod into the dock. Nobody understood angst better than Nina Simone and Norah Jones. Before she could give in to her funky mood completely, a loud knock sounded at the front door. She decided to ignore it, but the knocking persisted and she gave in.

"Who is it?" Her voice sounded every bit as irritable as she was.

"It's me, Alexis. Let me in before your neighbors call the law on me."

She was so startled at hearing Jared's voice that she opened the door immediately. She was surprised to see that he looked as bad as she felt. His hair was mussed, he hadn't shaved and he had an expression on his face that she'd never seen before; he looked both tired and furious.

"Can I come in?"

Alexis waved a hand to allow him to enter, but she didn't say anything. Jared looked down at her with a frown. "What did that woman say to you? I saw you leaving the building and you looked like you were ready to kick someone's behind, so I know you ran into her. What did she say?"

"She didn't have to say much. When you walk in on a naked woman, there isn't a lot to discuss," Alexis said crisply.

"Naked? She was naked in my loft? I should have called the cops."

"What did you do?"

"I fired her and tossed her out, what do you think I did?"

Jared had taken both of her hands and was walking backward, leading her over to the sofa. She resisted the automatic impulse to pull away from him because the touch of his warm skin was too enticing to ignore. Besides, his words had ignited her curiosity. "You fired her? I thought you were in some kind of relationship with her. Is that what you do when you're tired of a woman?"

They were now on the sofa and Jared was still holding her hands. His grip tightened for a moment before he laced his fingers in hers.

"Kellie was an executive sous chef in training. When I sent for reinforcements, Damon was supposed to come down here to help me with the hiring and training, but his kids got sick and he sent that moron instead. She's actually a competent chef but she's obviously crazy. Even after she asked me over that one time and I'd made myself perfectly clear, Lucas tried to tell me that she still had a thing for me, but she was always professional at work. I guess she thought this was her big chance to lay it all on the line or something because she got access to my house key and copied it. She was standing in my living room looking like I was supposed to be happy she was there."

Jared's voice grew cold as he recalled the scene in his loft and he let go of her hands. "I mean, there she was, grinning like an idiot, like she was the hottest thing in the world and I was supposed to be overcome with lust or something."

He rose abruptly and started walking around the room with the residual anger radiating from him so strongly it was almost visible. "I could have lost everything because of one horny woman," he fumed. "I invited my neighbor to come over for a beer and we sat there drinking and talking about nothing while she got her stuff together and left."

Alexis had to ask, "Why did you ask your neighbor over?"

"For a witness. I wanted someone to see her clothed with no bruises or marks on her body and no force used in any way. If that nitwit decides to try and turn the tables on me, who's gonna take my word over hers? I had to call my brother to make sure he knows she's a) crazy and b) fired. I had to get the locks changed at the restaurant and at the loft. I had to call my lawyer and the human resources person at corporate," he said wearily. "It's been one hell of a day. I came home early to surprise you and I end up getting a real nasty surprise of my own which led to hours of cussing and yelling and covering my behind. But the most important thing I had do was make sure that you weren't embarrassed or hurt by anything that heifer did or said to you. You weren't, were you?"

"Yes, I was," Alexis said bluntly.

Jared's look of disappointment was hard for her to take, but Alexis was determined to get all her feelings out in the open. He stopped pacing around and sat down next to her, putting his arm around her shoulders.

"How would you have felt if you'd come in here and there was a man wearing nothing but a towel and acting like he'd just gotten out of the bed with me? Would you have liked that?"

"Hell, no. As a matter of fact I'd be locked up right about now, trying to get somebody to post bail because things would've gotten real ugly real fast," Jared answered her frankly. "You probably haven't realized this about me, but I can be pretty possessive. What's mine is mine and I have no intentions of sharing you with anyone else on this earth, beauty."

It would have been a good time for a long, mind-bending kiss if they were the leads in a romantic comedy, but this was the real world and Alexis couldn't allow herself to get swept up in the moment. She forced herself to not melt into his embrace and crossed her arms tightly as if to hold back the yearning she was feeling for his warmth.

"That sounded really sweet, Jared, but we have to face facts. I barely know you and after today, I realized just how little I know about you and your life away from here. You should have a pretty good idea of how hurtful it was to see some blonde Amazon dripping water on your floor wearing nothing but a towel and my bracelets."

His face turned red and his voice was louder than she'd ever heard it. "She had on your bracelets? Are you telling me that she had the nerve to put on your jewelry like she owned it? That's what I'm talking about, the witch is crazy. That's why I had somebody come into the loft while she was there because Kellie has some screws loose that nobody paid any attention to. I've never given that woman any reason to think that I'm interested in her yet she comes down here with a stolen key, lets herself into my home and tries to steal my woman's jewelry, like I left it there for her. I try never to use the word *bitch* because my mother taught me better than that, but if you look up the word in the dictionary, there'd be a picture of that woman with all her capped teeth showing. How could you have believed anything she said?" He was clearly hurt, which annoyed Alexis instead of reassuring her.

"Look, I barely know you and we've gotten way too intimate way too soon, so how was I supposed to know she wasn't your real girlfriend? It's not like she had a flashing sign over her head saying *crazy broad*," Alexis snapped. "For all I know you could have a whole houseful of bleached blondes waiting for you in Chicago. Just because you latched onto me doesn't prove anything except that you're horny."

Jared drew back as though she'd slapped him and to tell the truth, her words were so harsh she may as well have accompanied them with a smack across his face. She was aware that she might have gone too far and she braced herself for what was sure to be an ugly argument. But once again, Jared surprised her. He stared at her for a long moment before speaking, but he found the right words.

"Look, Alexis, I will agree that our relationship has been brief and extremely hot, but that doesn't make it any less real, at least on my part. You had no way of knowing who or what that crazy wench was up to and I can't blame you for being upset. If the shoe had been on my foot, I'd be a lot madder than you are right now. A whole lot madder. Like I said, I'd be in the county lockup right now. I'm asking you to take me on faith and for you to just assume that I'm the kind of guy I say I am, which is asking a lot." He stopped talking and pulled her closer to his body, taking her hand.

"I think I'm going to have to prove myself to you and show you that I'm a man who's worthy of your trust. I can show you better than I can tell you, so that's what I'm going to do."

Alexis was trying vainly to think of the perfect, sophisticated rejoinder, but words failed her. "What do you mean?"

Jared put both his arms around her and held her close. "I mean I'm going to show you my heart and prove that this is something real, that's what I mean." He kissed her gently on her temple before capturing her mouth. The sensation of being joined with him once again was mesmerizing. Before she knew what was happening, she was in Jared's lap kissing him as if there was no tomorrow. There was nothing between them except her soft silk pajamas and she could only think about getting rid of them as soon as possible, but he had other ideas. As quickly as she ended up in his lap, she was back on the sofa and he was standing.

"What are you doing?" she asked in confusion.

"I'm getting ready to go home," he announced. "I'm going to prove to you that I'm not just some horny letch trying to get over on you and that means I'm taking myself home. I'm going to take you out tomorrow to a movie and a nice dinner and I'm going to church with you on Sunday, so how about you walk me to the door and we'll talk later."

Alexis was stunned as she allowed Jared to lead her to the door, but she was gratified by one last burning kiss before he left. "You'll see, beauty. You'll never have anything to worry about when you're with me. Never."

She locked the door after he left and leaned against it while she thought about everything he'd said. He could show her better than he could tell her, he'd said. Some convincing was just what she needed. She went right to bed, but she had a lot to think over before sleep claimed her.

Chapter 17

Jared meant exactly what he'd said on Friday night; they had a very nice date on Saturday but nothing else. She was pleased that he was taking his vow to show her what she meant to him seriously, but she was honest enough to admit that she missed their red-hot lovemaking. It was a wonderful date and Jared was as attentive and charming as he always was, but he took her home and left after just a few kisses. That was a good way for him to prove he was truly interested in her, but he was such a passionate lover that she truly missed his touch. However, there was no point in thinking about it now since it was Sunday morning and time for church, which gave her plenty to ponder without adding hot sex to the mix.

He'd had agreed to go to church with her with no hesitation and now the day of reckoning was here. She'd deliberately not mentioned the invitation again to see if he'd forget or try to wiggle out of it, but he hadn't. In fact, he'd reminded her after he drove her home on Saturday night. He'd said, "I'll pick you up tomorrow morning. Are we going to the eight o'clock service or the later one?"

Alexis normally liked going to the early service because it had the advantage of always ending on the dot. It had to, in order for the regular service to start on time at ten-thirty. Because she couldn't face dragging Jared out of bed at the crack of dawn to get ready since he'd been working so hard, they were going to the later service. So now it was Sunday morning and she was dressed and ready to go. The African Methodist Episcopal church she and her family had attended since she was a baby had a relaxed dress policy, but Alexis still liked dressing up on Sunday. She had a vast wardrobe of ultra-nice clothes and if she didn't wear them, they'd languish in the closet, in peril of falling out of style. Besides, she wanted to look nice for Jared.

She chose a black pencil skirt with a raspberry silk top and a matching belted jacket paired with black platform pumps that had an ankle strap to show off her toned, shapely legs. She had just finished slipping on her gold bangle bracelets when she heard Jared's knock at the door. She was walking to the door when a thought made her stop in midstride. She hadn't said anything about attire and she wondered if he'd be wearing a suit or one of his nice sweaters and jeans. Her heart skipped a beat when she saw that he was wearing a beautiful navy suit that had to be custom-tailored, given his height. His crisp shirt matched his eyes and the silk shantung tie was the same color. Jared looked just like a model for some expensive men's cologne or a luxury car.

"Good morning, good-looking," she said sweetly.

He smiled down at her and kissed her on the cheek. "Good morning, Alexis. That color is beautiful on you. Ready to go?"

"Yes, if you'll put my necklace on. I always chip a nail on the clasp."

Jared took the thick gold chain and put it around her neck

before fastening it easily on the first try. There was something so familiar about the gesture it made her eyes tear up a bit. It was as though they'd been together for years and this was just part of their normal Sunday-morning routine. Jared didn't notice her tiny shift in mood. They talked about nothing in particular until they reached the church parking lot. Alexis reflected on something the great Dr. Martin Luther King, Jr. had once said as she waited for Jared to open the car door for her. He'd said that 11:00 a.m. on Sunday morning was the most segregated hour in America, due to the fact that blacks and whites simply didn't worship together. It wasn't as true now as when he'd said it, but there was a lot of truth in his words. People of all colors attended Hightower AME, her home church, but not in any great numbers. Jared certainly stood out among the congregation after they took their seats, but mostly because of his height and his cover-model good looks.

She studiously avoided looking at the choir stand where her mother was singing with the Gospel Chorus. Sherri and Sydney joined them with Sydney sitting between her mother and Alexis as always. She wondered if she needed to explain anything about the service to Jared, but to her surprise he was perfectly comfortable. From the moment Reverend Johnson proclaimed, "This is the day the Lord has made, let us rejoice and be glad in it," Jared proved himself to be not only comfortable but fluent in Methodism. He sang all the words to every hymn without consulting the hymnal; he seemed to anticipate the order of service and knew all the words to The Apostles' Creed by heart. He also showed no hesitation in standing up when the visitors were recognized.

This was a quaint custom that Alexis despised. Whenever she went to church with a friend and the hospitality committee coerced the visitors to stand up and introduce themselves to the congregation, Alexis would either head for the ladies room before the event or sit like a statue and pretend as if it wasn't her first time in the pew. She hated the homey tradition and would cheerfully have taken a hot poker in her ear rather than do it. For this reason, she rarely ventured from her home church. But Jared was just as suave and debonair as always.

"Good morning, young man. What is your name and what brings you here this morning?"

"Good morning. I'm Jared VanBuren and I was invited by Ms. Alexis Sharp. I'm very happy to be here in your welcoming church on this beautiful Sunday morning."

"And where is your church home, Mr. VanBuren?"

"I attend Vesper Park United Methodist Church in my hometown of Chicago."

That explained a lot to Alexis; the United Methodist church was very similar to the African Methodist Episcopal church in many ways. Another coincidence of commonality between them, or *fate,* as Jared would say.

Reverend Johnson smiled widely. "I know the pastor of your church, he's a fine man of God."

"Yes, sir, he is. I'll certainly let him know that I had the privilege of being here."

It might have gone on forever if the reverend's wife hadn't discreetly cleared her throat to signal him to wind it up. Church was about to be dismissed and the rev and Jared were just chattin' away like fraternity brothers. There was no point in trying to flee right after service for several reasons. It was childish to run off; it wasn't going to happen, anyway, because Alexis could see Alana sauntering over to them, and most important, because Jared wanted to meet her mother. *It's nice that one of us is a civilized adult,* she thought.

They lingered in the vestibule while waiting for Aretha to take off her choir robe and join them. While they waited, Jared got acquainted with Sydney, who was most impressed with him. Despite her young age, she was a budding gourmet and self-professed foodie who watched the Food Network on weekends, the only time she got to watch television. She shook Jared's hand with the aplomb of a debutante and informed him that she knew who he was.

"I've seen you on the Food Network. You're a famous chef."

While she and Jared talked, Alana corralled Alexis and gave her an approving look. "I'm going to give him an A plus," Alana said. Alexis opened her mouth to answer but Aretha appeared, looking outstanding in a winter white suit with taupe accessories.

"Alexis, aren't you going to introduce me to your young man?"

"Of course I am. Mama, this is Jared VanBuren. Jared, please meet my mother, Mrs. Aretha Sharp."

Aretha extended her hand and Jared took it with a slight bow. "Mrs. Sharp, it's an absolute pleasure to meet you at last."

Ava finally joined them from wherever she'd been sitting in the large church. Jared looked at them all, Aretha, Alana, Alexis and Ava, and looked suitably impressed with their beauty and style. "It sounds like a cliché, Mrs. Sharp, but I can certainly see where your daughters inherited their beauty."

"How sweet," Aretha said. She was trying to be aloof, but she was very favorably disposed to Jared. When he took the coat that was over her arm and held it so she could slip it on, it was all over. She might not be a fan of most men, but tall, good-looking and well-mannered was a potent combination, even for Aretha.

Alana winked at Alexis and whispered, "Another A plus. Very smooth, sis."

Sherri's brown eyes were lit up with glee as she and Alexis put the finishing touches on dinner. Alexis was still unsettled from the events at church, and after. Sherri was sympathetic but amused.

"Honestly, have you ever seen Mama that bowled over by anyone, male or female? If she hadn't a previous engagement for dinner, we'd all be sitting down together because Jared wanted to take us all out."

Instead, Sherri had invited them to dinner at her house and they'd happily accepted. Jared and Sydney were playing some noisy game on Wii in the living room as Alexis and Sherri set the table and tossed the salad while the corn muffins baked. Sherri pointed out that it could have been much worse.

"Jared is a lovely man and I think he won over the entire church this morning. And I've been telling you for years that you don't really understand your mother as well as you think you do. She's a handful, I'll grant you that. But she's a very well-educated woman with a good head on her shoulders."

It was true; Aretha Sharp was in charge of the Public Health department for the city of Columbia and she was good at what she did.

"When your mother started seeing the statistics about the relationship between the crack epidemic and the rise of birth defects and addicted babies, especially in this county, she took it seriously. She devoted more time and effort than anyone in the state to educating people about it. And when HIV and AIDs came along, your mother was a tiger. She never did see it as a so-called gay disease. She knew what it could mean for young women, especially women of color and she was once again right. Your mother, in her own overly protective way, merely brought her crusade home. She was trying to protect her girls from the vagaries of life by making sure you didn't fall through the cracks of society into the arms of some seedy jerk."

Alexis stood back with her hand on her hip. She always

knew that Sherri and Aretha adored each other, but this was a long and passionate speech for Sherri to be making in defense of the Queen, as she and her sisters often called their mother.

"Sher, she could have brought home some pamphlets or a DVD or something. She didn't have to make up a family curse, for the love of God."

Sydney ran through the kitchen to see if dinner was ready. "Don't take the Lord's name in vain, Aunt Alexis," she chided.

She looked so much like her mother had as a child that Alexis had to stifle a laugh. She was also fair skinned with auburn hair, but hers was in long braids. She wore big round glasses that made her even cuter than she already was.

"Out of the mouths of babes," Alexis said. "You're right, Sydney, that was very wrong of me. Are you having fun with Jared?"

"Oh, yes. But I'm beating him," she said gleefully.

Sherri laughed. "See? He's won another heart. I'm going to let this go, but your mother wasn't the one who invented the curse myth. It was your great aunt. You should ask your mom about it instead of assuming the worst. Just remember, her methods were unorthodox but they worked. You and Alana and Adrienne are all successful, independent women, although we never see Adrienne since she moved to California. Is she ever coming home?"

"For Christmas, she says, but you never know. And where does my beloved baby sister fit into this picture of independence and success?"

"Oh, Lexie, Ava's a work in progress. Anyway, I have to tell you that you and Jared make a beautiful couple. He looks at you like Barack looks at Michelle. It makes my heart race and I'm not the recipient of his warm, loving gaze. It's just like I told you before, he's your Poetry Man," she teased.

Alexis smiled at her friend. "You're not going to believe

this, but Jared has a tattoo on his foot." She told Sherri about it and watched her eyes grow wide with surprise.

"I told you so. Go get your man, honey, dinner's ready."

Chapter 18

Jared couldn't remember a more relaxing Sunday. It had been a while since he'd been to church with his whole family, and he'd enjoyed the service and especially meeting Alexis's mother. Meeting Sydney had been an event in itself. She was an exceptionally smart and well-behaved child and adorable, to boot. A nice Sunday dinner of home-cooked food and now he and Alexis were in jeans, relaxing on her comfortable sofa watching the game with a fire going. Well, one of them was watching the game; Alexis was curled up on top of him, sleeping soundly. This was why his mother was constantly after him to settle down. This was contentment to the highest degree.

He'd never given marriage any thought because he was too busy living his life. He'd spent his time pursuing his own interests and keeping his relationships free and easy. He wanted to do as he liked with no entanglements and he tried to seek out like-minded women who weren't looking for someone to put a ring on it. But even when a woman professed to be totally immersed in her career with no desire for domesticity, he found that after a few weeks of dating they were ready to call the wedding planner. Since meeting Alexis, his perspective had changed.

She was the first person he wanted to see in the morning and the last one at night. Like most men, he hated talking on the phone unless he was talking to her. He liked the way she could understand his work habits, since she was also self-employed and loath to give up the iron reins of control over her businesses. And he loved the fact that she, like he, was figuring out that it was no way to live and was working out a better business model. Alexis was smart, sunny, playful and gorgeous. On top of everything else, she was the most amazing lover he'd ever had. It was impossible to think about ever being with another woman.

He tried to return his attention to the game, but the warmth of Alexis's womanly curves and the soft, feminine fragrance that drifted up to his nostrils made it difficult to concentrate on a bunch of big hairy gladiators slamming into each other on the playing field. His thoughts keep traveling around in a totally different sphere. He was picturing Alexis in his house in Chicago, on the beach in Aruba or Hawaii, in the audience when he appeared on *Iron Chef America* after the first of the year. He wondered if she'd like traveling with him to do public appearances; he'd been offered a contract for a series of shows on Food Network. Even in her sleep, Alexis could seduce him; her hips moved against him and he wondered how long it would be before they made love.

As if she was telepathic, Alexis came awake with a soft little sigh and shifted her body over his in a long, sensual stretch. "Who's winning?" she murmured.

Jared ran his hands up and down her pliant curves, palming her rounded behind before he slid them up under her top to caress her back. "I am," he answered.

They were both laughing as they undressed each other in the bedroom. They'd started kissing and one thing led to another and in their haste to exit the sofa, Alexis had knocked over a bowl of pistachios which were still waiting to be retrieved. She compounded her antic by stepping on one and yelping from pain. Jared had put an end to it by throwing her over his shoulder and carrying her out of the room, which made her dissolve in giggles.

Their laughter faded as the clothes disappeared. Alexis was on her knees between his thighs while he sat on the side of the bed. She put her hands under his jersey and rubbed his chest with her palms while he pulled the shirt over his head with lightning speed. She continued to move her palms in circles, using her thumbs to tease his flat nipples to attention.

"You are a gorgeous man, Jared," she purred. Her hands moved up to his shoulders as she leaned forward and licked his lower lip, then the upper, circling his mouth until he eagerly parted his lips and their tongues mated, gliding over each other in a long kiss that made their level of desire rise and grow as if there were flames licking at their bodies. She slid her fingers into his thick hair and held on, prolonging their kiss until he began to return the favors.

Jared removed her top, tossing it in the direction of the slipper chair upholstered in a hydrangea print fabric. She caught her breath as he admired her breasts in her delicate half-cup bra the color of peonies. His fingertips followed the curve of her breasts before running his tongue down her cleavage as he unfastened the front clasp to reveal them, ripe and ready for his loving. She gasped with pleasure as his lips and tongue worked their magic on her nipples, making them swell and blossom into hardened buds of passion in his mouth. He didn't hurry; he took his time and lavished each one with his tongue, holding her hips as she began to rock with fever from the searing sensation that was building between her legs.

She started making the incredibly sexy sounds she always uttered when they made love while Jared unzipped her jeans and pulled them down along with the lacy thong that matched her bra. Once she was freed of all her clothing, he followed suit and got rid of his jeans and briefs to stand before her with his huge hardness ready for her. She put both her hands around its weight and held him so he could put on the condom. When he was ready they changed places so that he was on the bed. He turned her around and guided her back to him, his hands on her hips as he positioned her so that he could enter. He rubbed the tip against her, feeling how wet she was and he pushed, filling her completely.

The new position increased the pleasure for Alexis, driving her to a height she'd never reached so quickly. She rode him hard, squeezing him tightly as the waves shimmering over her body turned into a hard, pulsing throb. Jared held her hips, loving the look of her perfect brown globes as she rode him. The sight of his manhood penetrating her aroused him even more and he pumped harder, long strokes to bring her more satisfaction. His pleasure grew as quickly as hers, mounting until a final tightening of her body on his brought him to a volcanic climax that rocked every bit of his being.

Soon they were in each other's arms, locked together on the bed, both of them sweaty and hot and satisfied. Jared kissed her again with great tenderness and smiled. "Best. Day. Ever."

Alexis couldn't have agreed with him more.

Chapter 19

"So what do you want for your birthday, beauty?"

"I want not to have a surprise party." Alexis's voice was muffled as she pulled an old Indiana University sweatshirt of Jared's over her head.

They were in his big bed at the loft and despite his insistence that he could keep her warm, she was chilly. The temperature had taken a dip as November progressed and even though Jared declared the weather to be springlike, Alexis was always cold at his place with its fourteen-foot-high ceilings, brick walls and giant windows.

Now that she was covered to midthigh with the soft, well-worn sweatshirt, she dove under the covers to snuggle up in Jared's willing arms.

"You don't want a birthday party? I thought everyone wanted one," Jared said before kissing her neck.

"I don't want a surprise party. My staff gets together with Sherri and my sisters and every year they come up with something outlandish and crazy. It's fun," she admitted, "but I don't really like a big honking party. They do it every year and they usually scare the crap out of me when they jump up and yell surprise. I think they're trying to give me a heart attack."

"I think you're on your own, babe. I've met most of your staff and they are some highly creative and eccentric individuals. Especially that Margo. I'm kinda scared of her."

Alexis shouted with laughter at his remark. She had a richly varied group of employees at both locations and Margo was truly an original. She had several facial piercings and she looked quite Goth with her blue-streaked black hair, thickly kohl-rimmed eyes and black lipstick, which contrasted sharply with her snow-white skin. She was an amazing massage therapist and she was always booked solid, so Alexis didn't care how she looked.

"You don't know Margo. She's as gentle as a kitten and she's very sweet. She dresses that way to feel brave. She's a sweetie."

"That would be you," he countered. "Now, since I have no control over your party, tell me what you want for your birthday."

She propped up herself on one elbow and gazed down at him. "Jared, I don't need another single thing. You've given me so many lovely things that I couldn't ask you for more."

It was true; Jared was both generous and creative. When he came back from New York, he'd brought her sinfully expensive Jo Malone candles and perfume. He kept his word about the Hanky Panky panties and bought her a dozen pair in luscious colors. When he discovered that she liked musical theater and old movie musicals, he bought her something that brought tears to her eyes. He gave her a book called *Remember How I Love You,* a book which consisted of the poems the late Broadway great Jerry Orbach had written to his wife every day of their marriage. Considering her love of poetry, it was a touching gift, especially since he also wrote her little poems and left them on her pillow, on the refrigerator door, the bathroom mirror and even under her windshield wiper.

"You never ask me for anything, which makes it all the more fun for me to give you things. And since it's the first birthday I'll be celebrating with you, I want it to be special."

"It will be special, the most wonderful birthday ever. All I need is you."

"Better be careful what you wish for. You could be stuck with me for the rest of your life and then what would you do?"

"Be happy." Before her face flamed up from blurting it out, his mouth covered hers and she didn't have to talk or explain, just enjoy.

Despite her protests, Jared had a surprise for Alexis on her birthday. He had several of them, as a matter of fact. Now that his project was back on schedule, he could plan things out in a more orderly fashion which was a great help, personally and professionally. It was a good thing since her birthday was the week before Thanksgiving and the soft opening of Seven-Seventeen was scheduled for the first week of December. He had a lot on his plate but he had no doubt he could handle it all.

As she'd predicted, she was given a surprise party but this one was a real surprise. Alexis got a phone call from the security company to alert her that something was wrong with the alarm at Sanctuary Two. This was vexing because it was a new system and it wasn't supposed to be malfunctioning. Besides that, it was barely dawn on freakin' Friday morning, her day to sleep late because she was taking the weekend off. And Jared was out of town, which made her cranky because she missed him like mad. He'd be back the next day, but at the moment she was just royally ticked off.

She threw on a fleece jogging suit that she never wore out

of the house, thrust her feet into a pair of fuzzy slippers that looked like boots and zipped up a leather coat that she'd had since the dawn of time. The only time she wore it was when she was raking the yard in cold weather but she didn't care about looking fashionable, she just wanted to get the ordeal over with. Swearing under her breath, she drove to Sanctuary Two as fast as possible without attracting the attention of the police and pulled up next to the employee entrance. She didn't see the security company or the police so she assumed that they were in the front of the building. Nothing seemed amiss to her as she entered the proper code into the panel. She pushed open the door leading to the public part of the spa so she could go to the front door and then she jumped a foot into the air as a chorus of voices screeched "SURPRISE!"

There they all were, dressed in sweats, bathrobes and pajamas, her ever-loving mischief-making staff, plus Sherri and Alana. All she could do was laugh and accept hugs, good wishes presents and some really good pastry. They'd made a brunch for her that was set up in the yoga studio with pretty decorations and music playing.

"You got me again, you crazy people! I love you all so much," she said with tears running down her face. It was a tradition; no matter how much she protested, she loved their thoughtfulness and she always cried.

"Oh, don't cry," a deep, dear and familiar voice said.

She whirled around to see Jared standing there looking exhausted but very happy to be where he was.

He put his arms around her and kissed her, right in front of God and everybody. A loud chorus of "whoo-hoo" and "get it, get it" rose up from her crew, but she didn't even hear.

"I thought you weren't coming back until tomorrow," she whispered.

"I couldn't stay away. We drove all night because we couldn't miss this," he said with a secretive smile.

She was so glad to see him she missed what he was saying at first, and then it hit her. "We? Who is we?"

A big box wrapped in pink paper with a huge ribbon was on the table he led her to and he urged her to take off the lid. She did so and her eyes grew huge at the sight of two Welsh Corgi puppies, each wearing a big lavender bow. She covered her mouth with both hands and looked at Jared.

"Are you serious? These are really for me? You aren't kidding me, are you?"

Jared laughed at her gently as she scooped up one puppy and then the other, cuddling them both to her cheeks. "Of course I'm not kidding you. These are your babies, beauty."

Margo was completely taken with them, reaching out to touch their soft fluffy coats as they licked Alexis's cheeks, chin, and ears, whatever they could reach. "They're so cute! What are their names?" she asked Jared.

He was amazed at her voice; it was soft and sweet like a child. "Whatever Alexis wants to name them, they're all hers."

One puppy was mostly black with a white face and touches of tan, and the other was golden brown and white. "This is Sookie," Alexis said, "and the golden one is Honeybee."

Jared gave a mock groan. Everything about Alexis was perfect except for her love of country music, especially Blake Shelton.

The puppies apparently liked their names and yipped their approval. When she could finally let them go, Alana took one and Margo took the other so that Alexis could mop her eyes which were again leaking tears of joy. It was by far the best birthday party she'd ever had and it wasn't over. When they had a moment alone, Jared told her that their real celebration was going to be that night at the loft and it would just be for the two of them.

Alexis finally noticed a stranger, a big man standing quietly by the door. He was huge with a red undertone to his medium-brown skin. He was about Jared's height but where Jared was long and lean this one was heavily muscled and built like a linebacker.

"Who is he?"

"This is my best friend, Roland Casey. Roland, this is Alexis."

Roland grinned, revealing big white teeth that looked like a toothpaste ad. "I've heard a lot about you, Alexis. A lot. About you. All about you," he said in a warm, teasing tone.

Jared ignored his friend's pointed remark and put his arm around Alexis. "Roland will be here for a while. He's not only training the new managers, but he'll be working with the culinary school, too."

"So nice to meet you, Roland. I hope we can make you welcome here in Columbia."

An excited yip made her turn around to see Sookie and Honeybee chasing after Alana. Alexis excused herself from the two men and went to bond with her babies. She began opening her birthday gifts, which were all dog-related. Puppy Chow, doggie sweaters, doggie shampoo and every dog toy and accessory imaginable let Alexis know that her people had been in on her surprise, which was even more endearing.

"I told you she was beautiful, didn't I," Jared said to Roland.

"She's everything you've been saying she is. I thought for a while that you'd lost your mind but I see that you found someone really special. Miracles do happen," he said, moving out of the way as Jared aimed a punch at his huge shoulder.

Roland took another look at Alexis's animated face and joyous smile as she sat on the floor and played with the puppies. She really was a beauty, no doubt about it.

"So, Jared, she got any sisters at home?"

Roland couldn't understand why Jared was laughing so hard; it wasn't that funny.

The rest of her celebration was just as much fun, although a bit more formal. Jared wanted to prepare a sit-down dinner for her at the loft, as opposed to their casual meals, and he was making her something special. When he'd asked what she might like, she'd given him a smile full of mischief.

"There's something that I want to eat more than anything and I've never tasted it," she told him. "Wait just a sec, let me show you."

She'd fetched her tattered copy of *The Nero Wolfe Cookbook,* a wonderful volume with almost every recipe for the gourmet dishes that the esteemed Rex Stout had written about in the Nero Wolfe detective series. She presented it to Jared and showed him the recipe for something called Saucisse Minuit.

"I don't know if it's a real dish or if it's something Mr. Stout invented," she said. "He was quite a cook himself. But the way he wrote about food was just amazing. I've wanted to taste this for years. Can you make this for me?"

Jared looked at her and shook his head slightly. "You read about this in a book and you want me to make it just so you can taste it? That's how I can tell someone who really appreciates good food—someone who's curious about the preparing and serving and creating of a good meal. You astound me every day, Alexis. You're perfect. Too good to be true," he'd told her.

"That's sweet, honey, but can you make this or not? Playing with my food is like playing with my emotions," she warned him.

It was a complicated recipe because it didn't have any specific measurements. It called for pheasant, goose and pork as well as wine and brandy and a slew of spices, including roasted pistachio nuts. Plus, it was a sausage that required casing. Jared thought it would be a snap, but he let her think it was going to be extremely difficult.

She arrived at his loft looking like a beauty queen even though she was casually dressed in a soft cream-colored Italian-made sweater with a huge cowl that slipped off her shoulder with a matching pair of thick leggings. The puppies were thrilled to see their mommy again; Jared had decided to keep them overnight because he had also bought all their equipment. Beside the gifts she'd gotten at the party, Jared had bought crates, pillows, toys and dishes for the two of them. He'd remembered everything.

Alexis finally remembered to kiss him hello and tell him how handsome he looked, which he did in dress slacks and a cashmere pullover sweater in an aqua-blue color that set off his eyes. He showed her the table which was set beautifully with a black table runner, black napkins, gold chargers and square white plates. Everything looked perfect, right down to the Taittinger champagne chilling in a bucket and the deep red roses in the center between the white candles.

After she washed her hands and he seated her at the table, they began to dine on the sumptuous meal he'd made, starting with caviar crepes with crème fraiche on the side. It was so delicious she moaned out loud. The main course was simply astounding; the plump, crisply browned Saucisse Minuit surpassed all her expectations. It just melted in her mouth. He'd kept it simple, serving the sausages with polenta and *haricots verts,* delicate fresh green beans. Watercress salad followed with a champagne vinaigrette that was so light and delicious she wanted to lick the plate. She was much too full for the dessert he'd made, which was a flourless chocolate cake made with ground pistachios and a raspberry coulis, but he assured her that they could eat it whenever.

"The way I want to eat it involves you being naked, so it needs to wait until later, anyway," he said with the sexy smile that drove her crazy.

Jared refused any help in clearing up, so Alexis played with her puppies. She sat right on the floor and wrestled with the little girls, laughing like a child. She still couldn't get over the fact that he'd gone to Chicago, picked up the puppies from the breeder and driven all night to get back in time for her party. When he joined her and her new loves on the rug in front of the fireplace, she was dabbing at her eyes, overcome with emotion. He kissed away her tears and pleaded with her not to cry.

"You have no idea what that does to me, Alexis. If someone made you cry, really cry, I might have to go to jail over it because I couldn't let him live," he joked.

"Jared, you make me feel so special," she said softly. "I've never known a man like you."

He gently stroked her face. "That's because I'm one of a kind. I was made for you, just like you were made for me. We're a perfect pair."

She sighed with happiness, but he wasn't finished. "Speaking of perfect pairs," he drawled, "how do you like these?"

He presented her with a pair of diamond studs that were two carats each. With a matching necklace; a gold chain with a diamond that equaled the earrings.

"Jared, these are so beautiful," she said breathlessly.

"Not as beautiful as you are. You're what I think of when I hear the word *beauty*." He slipped three gold bangles on her wrist, each one spangled with tiny diamonds.

She was about to burst into more happy tears when Jared noticed the puppies turning around in the circles that were the puppy equivalent of the pee-pee dance. He got up quickly and headed for the door with a pup under each arm.

"Don't forget where we left off." He grinned as he left the loft.

Alexis wasn't going to forget anything about this day, this night or anything about the man she loved. A single tear ran down her cheek as she finally admitted that she was totally, utterly in love with Jared. It was a word he'd never used and she didn't know if he wanted to hear it but she wanted to shout it to the heavens. She wanted to put it on YouTube, Perez Hilton and TMZ, but at the same time she was just a little bit terrified. Here in the loft, things were perfect, but outside this perfect bubble, things could get strange. She said a little prayer that nothing would happen to burst that bubble.

Chapter 20

The next night Jared again proved himself to be Superman. The occasion was the annual dinner dance given by Aretha's sorority and attendance was mandatory for Alexis and her sisters, which meant that Jared was coming, too. Alana was thrilled about it; Alexis less so.

Alana wasn't having any doubts from her sister. "Girl, quit overthinking everything! I swear, Lexie, your mind must be like a big hamster cage with wild-eyed little critters running in circles all day long. Let it go, Alexis. Relax, release and whatever else it is you do in yoga. Namaste, okay? Jared will be just fine at the dance. What do you think is gonna happen? You think some old Que or Kappa is gonna try to take him out? Calm down and try to figure out what I'm going to wear. Can I borrow something from you?"

They were in Alexis's private styling area and Alexis was profoundly glad that Alana had the ability to talk in a low voice. She'd just given her sister a shampoo and blow-dry and she was now curling the thick mane. Alana was making her laugh so hard that she had to stop a few times.

"Yes, you can have anything in my closet if you just quit talking. Do you see all those irons over there? Do you know how hot they are? Keep fooling around and you'll find out."

After Alexis made Alana's shoulder-length hair look like shimmering silk, they went to her house in search of the perfect outfit from Alexis's closet. Alexis sat cross-legged on the bed—with Sookie and Honeybee—watching Alana sort through all her fanciest dresses. The puppies were running in circles and rolling over each other while Alexis gave advice.

"Don't you have anything black?"

"Not a thing. Black drains the color away from the face and makes dark drown skin look gray. I don't have anything navy or brown or gray, either. Here, try on this one. It'll look great on you."

Alana was admiring herself in a short purple dress. It had a boat neck and a full skirt with a wide belt of multicolored jewels that made her waist look tiny. "Which shoes?"

"None of these, your feet are a size bigger than mine. Wear those fuchsia ones of yours with the straps, or the black pumps. I have a beaded bag you can borrow, too."

"What are you wearing?" Alana asked as she continued to preen in front of the full-length mirror.

"It's a surprise. I'm not telling." Alexis grinned. "You'll see tonight. Now you need to go home and get ready because that's what I'm going to do." She batted her eyelashes and refused to say another word.

Alana joined her on the bed and the puppies tumbled over themselves to get to her. "I can wait until tonight to see it. Alexis, I'm so happy for you. You found your other half," she said. "Two halves are the only way to make a whole," she added.

Alexis picked up Honeybee, who was chewing her big toe. "Jared has a friend in town. His name is…"

Alana jumped off the bed so fast she scared Sookie. "You know I don't play that. I got the dress, I'll see you tonight, 'kay, thanks, bye," she said as she sailed out of the bedroom.

Alexis sighed as she looked at Sookie and Honeybee. "Your auntie Alana hasn't dated since her husband passed away. She's really scared," she told the dogs, who looked as if they understood every word. "But one of these days, she's going to find her other half, too." She rolled over laughing as her babies clambered on her to give her kisses.

When Jared saw what Alexis was wearing to the dance, they almost didn't make it out of the house. She had on a strapless red dress with a full skirt that fell below her knees, halfway to her slender ankles. The bodice was covered in heavy handmade French lace and the wide skirt, made of crepe-backed satin, swirled out and fell in silky folds. The sweetheart top of the dress followed the curve of her rounded breasts and the back dipped below her shoulder blades.

She wore black peep-toe pumps with a red platform and red four-inch heels and her only jewelry was the pieces Jared had given her. Her hair was gorgeous and her face glowed with a slight golden shimmer along her cheekbones. Smoky eyeshadow and liner made her eyes huge and dramatic, but her lips were luscious in a neutral shade with a bit of golden gloss.

"You take my breath away, Susanna" was all Jared said, in Langton Hughes fashion, after he saw her. "That dress is magnificent."

Alexis smoothed the front of the skirt. "Believe it or not, it belonged to my aunt BeBe. I had it cut off and the lace put on. And you're making me breathless, too. You're gorgeous, Jared." She gazed up at him in another perfectly tailored suit, this one black, with a crisp white shirt and a fantastic tie, black patterned in red and gold.

"Men aren't gorgeous," he countered.

"You are," she said.

"If you say so, I'm not going to argue with you. I want to get you out of here right now before we don't leave here for the next three days," he said hoarsely.

Everyone complimented the couple on their stunning appearance, especially Aretha who told Alexis that she'd never looked better. But the real compliments came when they started dancing. Jared was by far the best dancer Alexis had ever seen. There was a live band playing a variety of jazz and R&B and Jared moved his body to the music like nothing she'd ever imagined.

"Where in the world did you learn how to dance?"

Jared laughed at her surprise. "I'm from Chicago, beauty. It's a dancing town. If you can't dance, you can't get laid."

He could do everything from the stanky leg to the electric slide to the wobble dance and he did them all well. He took Aretha out on the floor and showed that he could also do regular ballroom dancing, which wowed all her friends. He ended up dancing with every member of her sorority, as well as Alana, Ava and Sherri. Practically every woman in the room wanted a dance with that handsome man. Alexis had to cover her mouth to keep in the giggles when she heard an older woman say how gorgeous he was.

"I thought George Clooney was the prettiest white man I ever saw, but this one has him beat," the older woman told her friend.

Alexis was sitting at the table with Aretha and they both heard the comment and when their eyes met, they burst into laughter.

"You're really happy, aren't you, baby?" Aretha's eyes were warm and loving as she looked at her daughter.

"I'm very happy, Mama."

"I like Jared. He's a good man, Alexis. A very good man."

Alexis was amazed by her mother's mellow about-face. "Who are you, lady, and what have you done with my mama? I've never heard you say a nice word about any man I've been involved with. Never. I've only been with Jared for what, a month, and you're singing his praises. What's going on?"

"Sweetie, chill." Aretha laughed as she saw the look on her daughter's face. "I'm sorry, Alexis. I know I've been hard on my girls, but I had a higher purpose in mind for you. You're everything you should be. You're smart and creative and independent and successful. It's time for you to find some lasting happiness and a lifetime love. I'm never wrong, honey. Jared is the man for you."

Alexis picked up her mother's glass and said, "What's in this juice?"

"You always were my smart-mouthed child," she said fondly.

"That was Alana, not me. Mama, if I ask you something, you'll tell me the truth, right?"

"If it's convenient and suits my purposes, yes."

"Mama!"

"Of course I will, sweetie."

"Are you and Daddy dating?"

Aretha's eyes widened and she smiled. "Ask him yourself. He just came in the door."

Alexis's mouth fell open as she saw Arthur Sharp, her tall, still-handsome father strolling over to Aretha as though there was nothing unusual about his appearance at the dance. He leaned down and kissed Aretha on her cheek and then gave one to Alexis.

"Daddy, what are you doing here?"

His dark eyes twinkled at her surprise. "I'm allowed to

leave Charleston, sweetie. I thought I'd better come meet your young man who your mother can't stop talking about."

And when Jared walked Alana back to the table, that's exactly what he did.

Jared and her father hit it off immediately and the evening just got better and better. Once Alexis recovered from the surprise of seeing her mother and father together in public, she and Jared danced all evening. That is to say at least they danced when he was available, because his dance card was quite full all night. He claimed her for one last slow dance and they looked into each other's eyes, talking without words. Being in the big ballroom which was already decorated for Christmas with thousands of white lights twinkling madly, made everything seem like it was touched by magic.

When they returned to Alexis's house after the dance, it still felt like a magical evening to her. They played with the sleepy puppies, drank champagne and made love, and everything seemed as if it was bathed in the same amber glow of the firelight.

They were talking quietly in bed before slipping into sleep. Jared told her how much he'd enjoyed meeting her father.

"He told me to call him Art," Jared reported. "You told me was a professor, but you didn't tell me he taught literature. That probably contributed to your love of poetry."

Alexis agreed sleepily. "He'd read to us all the time and he read a lot of poems. He used to give me books of poetry for my birthday and Christmas."

Like a shadow cast by moonlight, a random thought drifted across her consciousness and she asked Jared a question.

"Jared, are you going to keep the loft after Seven-Seventeen opens?"

"No, sweetheart, that's why I rented it. I'll be back in Chicago after it's up and running and I won't need it."

With those simple words, the very bottom fell out of Alexis's world and out of her heart, too.

Chapter 21

For the next few days, Alexis went on what she thought of as autopilot. She couldn't allow herself the luxury of falling to pieces; she had to keep going. Jared had never promised her anything and he'd never asked for anything that she wasn't willing to give him freely. He'd treated her better than any man had ever treated her in her life; he was sweet, kind, funny, generous, passionate and charming. She couldn't say that he'd taken anything away from her; he'd given her much more than she'd given him, than she could ever give him. So there was no reason for her to be heartbroken.

Sophisticated women did it all the time, didn't they? They took a lover and when it was over, there were no recriminations and no bad feelings. It was taking everything she had in the way of self-control to maintain her normal demeanor, but Alexis was determined not to make a fool out of herself before Jared went home to Chicago to live. The houses he had looked at on Hilton Head weren't for him; they were for his parents who were looking for a retirement home. It hadn't once crossed her mind that Jared's move to South Carolina was a temporary one, but it made sense. He had six restaurants up there; it was a growing empire, actually. How could he not live where his business was based?

She was sitting on the sofa, staring out the window and brooding while she watched the puppies playing. Her phone rang and she forced herself to sound normal when she answered it.

"Hi, Mama, what's up?" she said with false cheer.

"I'm fine, baby. I'm just calling to see how my grandpups are doing and to find out what you're bringing for Thanksgiving dinner. You and Jared are coming for dinner, aren't you?"

Alexis blinked hard. "Jared is going home to Chicago for his parents' anniversary. I think I told you that, or maybe I didn't. I'm not sure. What do you want me to bring for dinner? I'll make anything you want."

"Alexis Rochelle, what's the matter? You don't sound like yourself. Are you sick?"

"Yes, umm, no I'm not, Mama. Just cramps, that's all."

She was profoundly grateful that her mother bought the lie. Alexis was known for having excruciating cramps; that's why she'd been on birth control pills even while celibate. They helped control her hormonal output and relieve the pain.

"Well, drink some hot tea and let my grandpups lay on your tummy. They'll make you feel better. Why don't you bring dessert, Alexis? Make anything you want. And by the way, you know those cramps will go away after you and Jared have a baby."

Alexis almost choked at her mother's choice of words, but she managed to get off the phone without sobbing. She put the puppies on the sofa with her and they climbed into her lap and fell asleep within two minutes. Her mother was right, but not about having a baby. Maybe her great-aunt was correct; there really was a love curse on the women in her family and she was its latest victim.

It wasn't easy, but Alexis thought she was doing a grand job of being her usual bubbly self around Jared. He was so busy with the last-minute details of the soft opening that he wasn't as keenly tuned into her as usual or he'd have noticed a slight difference in her demeanor. He was taking the night off for the first time in days. Right now he was returning from walking the girls, as he called them. He was teaching them how to walk on their leads properly without chewing the end or lunging off after a random squirrel or chipmunk and they were learning very fast.

"We're back, goddess. The girls were very well behaved for the most part." He unclipped their leads from their harnesses and they barreled to Alexis as fast as their short little legs would carry them.

"I'm glad you're back, honey. Dinner is ready for you and for them," she said with a smile. She drank him in with her eyes, trying to add this to her catalog of memories. She'd started taking pictures of him constantly, not just the random cell phone shots of before; she was trying to keep every memory she would have of him pristine and perfect.

He was taking off his jacket but the kiss he gave her caught fire so quickly that it slipped to the floor. He hung it carelessly on the doorknob to the closet and put his arms around her for another kiss.

"Dinner smells wonderful. Is that some more of your spaghetti sauce?" Jared had been delighted to discover that Alexis made exceptional Italian food. She could make a Bolognese sauce that would fool an Italian grandmother into thinking it was from the old country.

"Yes, and I made meatballs for you, too."

Dinner was delicious and Jared ate with hearty appetite.

Something occurred to Alexis and she asked where Roland was. "He's welcome to come over for dinner anytime," she said.

Jared looked at her as if she'd offered him a fried bat meat sandwich. "No, he's not. He's my main man and everything but this is our time and I'm not sharing you. No way."

Alexis finally understood that Jared was feeling it, as well, the fact that they would soon be parting. It was too painful to think about but it was the only realistic thing to do. Jared talked about his brothers and sisters, but they'd never discussed his family in depth. It was just as well. The less she knew about them, the better. In her heart, although they had raised a wonderful son, she probably wasn't the daughter-in-law of their dreams. A sudden image of her dark face sitting at their Thanksgiving dinner table flashed before her eyes and the image was so incongruous it made her laugh out loud but the laughter was as bitter as tears.

Jared came from the kitchen to join her on the sofa. "What's so funny?"

She pointed at the puppies who'd managed to pull his coat down onto the floor and play tug-o'-war with a sleeve. He rescued the coat and dusted it off, telling them what naughty girls they were.

"Wanna go outside?"

That was the magic word they loved and they jumped up and down with excitement. Jared walked over to the sofa to give Alexis a quick kiss before taking them out and she managed to smile quite naturally.

"Hurry back. I'll have a surprise for you," she said mischievously.

"We'll run, in that case. Come on ladies, let's go."

Jared came back to a house that was considerably more serene than when he left it. He'd given the girls a good work-out and they were more than willing to go their crate and prepare for sleep, turning around in sleepy circles until they plopped on their pillows. He could hear the mellow voice of Kurt Elling coming from the bedroom and he followed it to its source. The room was lit with the Jo Malone candles and nothing else. A large towel was across the bed and Alexis was waiting for him wearing a red pair of the panties he loved and a matching bra that did wonderful things for her breasts. He started taking off his clothes as soon as he entered the room. He gathered her into his arms and kissed her.

"I was wrong. You make the bra look good, not the other way around."

"You're quite crazy. You do know that, don't you?"

He got on the bed next to her and pulled her on top of him. He would never get tired of the way she felt against him. That beautiful silky skin, the smell of her, the taste of her; everything came together in a perfect blend of beauty and sensuality that really did drive him crazy. She protested the new position mildly.

"You're supposed to be on your stomach. I'm giving you a massage," she told him. Her hand was already rubbing his chest, her fingernails teasing his nipple and sending a shiver all over his body.

"Suppose I want to make love to you? What do we do about that?"

"The activities aren't mutually exclusive, Jared. We can do both."

"If we do then I get to massage you first. I don't want you to be all tired out."

"You're the one who's been working the long hours," she countered. "You need this."

"No, I need this," he said, rolling over so that he was on top of her. He was an expert in unfastening her bras and in seconds she was bare to his loving lips and tongue. He knelt over her, giving her breasts the special touch that made her hips grind and her voice grow soft and sexy. She made the throaty purr he loved as he sucked and licked his way down her body while he pulled off her lace thong. He stroked her legs, putting them over his shoulders and licking his way down her thigh until he reached his goal, dipping into the sweet pool that was ready for him, the juices already flowing. His tongue found her treasure and he savored it like a rare gourmet treat, tasting it and sucking until she screamed his name.

He could feel her body's response, he felt the pulsing that let him know she was climaxing but he didn't stop. His tongue kept going and he kept feeding his desire until her hips were pumping and the throbbing between her legs grew stronger. With a final cry of pleasure her body tightened and released as he made his way back up her body and became one with her.

Nothing had ever felt so right as when he buried himself in her. She opened her legs wide for him, smiling up at him, giving him all of her as they joined. Every thrust brought them closer together until she started pumping, pulling everything from him. It was his turn to call her name in a hoarse chant that became a cry of pure passion as the most powerful sensation he'd ever felt rocked him into a climax like he'd never experienced in his life.

It was all Alexis, all about her and no one else. No one could come close to giving him what she did; not only in bed but in every way, every day, just by being the woman she was. They held each other tenderly and kissed as the aftermath of their loving turned into the warm and tender closeness he loved. He felt her body relax into sleep and before he joined her, he gave her a gift, one that he'd intended for Christmas. He just couldn't wait to give it to her another day.

Jared was moving as quietly as he could but Alexis still woke up when he was getting dressed. It was early in the morning and he was about to take the girls out for a walk.

"Good morning," she murmured. "You should let me take them so you can get some more rest."

He smiled and bent over to give her a kiss. "I'm fine, beauty. We'll be back in a few minutes."

She stretched like a cat, smiling as she felt the effects of their lovemaking all over her body. She got up with reluctance because she would much rather have stayed in bed and waited for Jared to come back, but she had to get up and get her day started. She went to the bathroom and tended to her most basic need first. When she was washing her hands after, she made an astounding discovery. There was a ring on the third finger of her left hand; a big oval diamond with small clusters of diamonds on either side of the center stone. She had to grip the vanity with her right hand because she was so stunned she lost her balance. When Jared came back in with Sookie and Honeybee, he found her sitting on the bed in a short red robe staring at her hand in wonder.

"Do you like it? I was going to wait until Christmas but I couldn't." He sat down next to her and pulled her into his lap, kissing her lightly on the lips. "I wanted to do this in a really romantic way, but after last night, I couldn't wait anymore. You told me you wouldn't believe I was your fiancé until I put a ring on it," he teased, "so now there it is.

"I want you to come home with me for my parent's anniversary. You would have met them when they come down here for the grand opening, but I want you to meet them now so we can be there for Thanksgiving," he said as though it was the most normal thing in the world. He finally noticed that she hadn't said a word.

"Alexis, you aren't talking. Don't you like the ring? It belonged to my grandmother and she gave it to me for my wife. If you don't like the setting we can change it, or we can get another one. Say something. Tell me what you're thinking."

She put her right hand over her left and held it there as

though she were protecting the ring. It took her a couple tries to get her voice working, but she was finally able to speak.

"Jared, I honestly don't know what to say. You tell me that you're moving back to Chicago and I thought that would be the end of us and now you're giving me a family heirloom and telling me you want me to come to your parent's celebration and Thanksgiving like it's no big deal. You calling me your fiancée was a little joke that started in the emergency room and now you're acting as though it was real. That's not how you start a marriage, Jared, especially one like ours."

She bit her lip and corrected herself. "Like ours would be if it was going to be." She looked as confused as her last sentence sounded, but Jared seemed to understand what she was talking about.

"Alexis, my love, I am often guilty of taking an idea and just charging ahead with it on my own and while it works for me most times, there are other times when it's not so successful. Like the Seven-Seventeen. Trying to take on the role of project manager and chef and owner and the rest of it was a recipe for disaster. I was doing too much and not communicating well and I learned a good lesson.

"I've been doing the same thing with you, I can see that. I just assumed that you knew how much I love you and how much I wanted to marry you. Everything was just clicking into place with us and we have so much in common that I knew it was fate. That I'd found the mate to my soul on a rainy street with a flat tire," he said with a tender smile. "Alexis, do you realize how rare that is, to look into a person's eyes and you know that this is the person you're going to be with for the rest of your life? From the moment I touched you, I felt it. When you were holding my hand in the emergency room, I knew. When we made love for the first time, it was like being handed a beautiful gift from the universe. There was no way I was ever going to let you go. No woman will ever be able to take your place in my heart, Alexis. You're it, that's all there is to it."

Tears were running down her cheeks but she was determined to have her say. "Jared, this is scary. This is crazy," she insisted. "You've never even told me that you love me."

"Not true. I told you every day in every way I could," he said gently. "And every time I made love to you, I would tell you, not just with my body, either. Every time, while you were going to sleep, I'd say I love you and you always said it back to me. You don't remember that?"

He wiped the tears from her eyes and kissed her again. She opened her hands to look at the ring again. It was beautiful. "Jared, I want to have a normal, happy family and that means I want to get along with my in-laws. You're acting like this is no big deal, but I want to be sure that they're going to love me and being forced on them during a big celebration and a big holiday isn't the best way to start out. I don't want to feel like the heroine in some dumb romantic comedy about an interracial marriage. I want it to be real and I want it to be right."

Jared surprisingly agreed with her. "Alexis, I understand what you're saying and, believe it or not, I understand how you're feeling. It's kind of like stepping out of the farmhouse into Oz, I know it is. I know in my heart that my family is going to love you as much as I do, but what I have to know is if you believe that I love you with all my heart."

"Yes," she said softly. "I do."

"Do you love me?"

"Yes, I really do."

"Then that's all that really matters. The rest of it we'll figure out together."

Chapter 22

Sherri rarely lost her temper but she was so shocked by what Alexis told her that she put both her hands on her hips and looked at her best friend as if she'd lost her mind.

"You did what? You let Jared just get on a plane and go home to Chicago without you when he made it perfectly plain that he loves you, wants to marry you and wants you to meet his family? What's the matter with you?"

Alexis shook her head, mute with misery. They were in her living room and she was sitting on the sofa with the puppies. They seemed to sense her mood and were trying their best to comfort her with licks and cuddles.

"Sherri, it was too much, I just couldn't think straight. He'd never said a word about wanting to get married or wanting me to meet his parents and then I wake up with a ring on my finger and a plane reservation in my name. How am I supposed to know what to do in a situation like that? You can't tell me that you would have acted any differently," she said defensively.

"We're not talking about me. We're talking about you and Jared. Stevie Wonder could see that the two of you are meant for each other. I don't care how unorthodox your courtship was, your connection is real. Really real. Even Sydney could see it and she's only six!"

Alexis's eyes were welling up with tears and Sherri relented, going from her standing position to sit with her and give her a hug. "I'm sorry to be so hard on you. I know this is scary. It's like free-falling from a plane in a way. But think about it. Do you think that some horrible racists could have raised a sweet Methodist boy to manhood and not know his heart? They have to be as kind and loving as he is because he'd never, ever let you walk into a den of lions ready to tear your little brown butt into shreds. Let me see that ring again," she said.

Alexis held out her trembling hand. "It was his grandmother's," she said softly. "Sherri, what should I do?"

"Follow your heart. You already know that Jared will defend you, protect you and treat you like a queen. Do you trust that he'll love you forever?"

"Yes."

"Then you're going to get dressed and I'm going to pack while you call Javier and tell him you're taking off until Monday. That's what you're going to do."

"What about Sookie and Honeybee?"

"Sydney will love having them stay with us. I'm on vacation and they'll have a ball with her. Quit stalling and get moving! And I'm calling Emily and Todd to pick you up from the airport and take you to Jared. Put some foot in it, chick, your man is waiting for you."

That's exactly what happened, too. Sherri was like a field marshal in her execution of the hastily thought-out plan. She had everything Alexis would need packed by the time she showered and dressed. Sherri whisked her to the airport and before she could really question the wisdom of what she was doing, Alexis was on a plane to Chicago. And when she got to the luggage claim area, there was Emily's smiling face. The sight of her filled Alexis's heart to the brim; she needed to see a familiar face to put everything into perspective for her.

Emily hugged her tight and said, "You've been busy, sister. Wanna tell me all about it?"

Alexis did, unburdening herself as they maneuvered through the terrible traffic at O'Hare Airport. They had plenty of time for Alexis to regale her with all the details of the whirlwind time she'd been with Jared. Almost all the details; there were some things that were too private to share. Emily seemed delighted instead of scandalized or judgmental. After all, she, too, had gone through the same type of whirlwind with Todd.

"You can be with someone for five years and have it be all wrong, and you can be with someone for five minutes and know that it's right. I think everything is going to work out perfectly and I agree with Sherri. There's no way that his parents could be awful. Todd knows Dr. VanBuren, he's the chief of staff at his hospital and he likes the man. Do you want to come home with me and freshen up?"

"Oh, absolutely. I want to see dem babies and I want to put on a dress. I can't go in there looking skanky," she said with a nervous laugh.

She was absolutely in love with Emily and Todd's babies by the time she left to go to the restaurant where the celebration was taking place. They were beautiful, chubby, healthy boys who looked just like their father. A sudden pang hit her as she thought about having Jared's babies someday. Emily had to forcibly drag her away from them long enough for her to take a quick shower, style her hair in a becomingly tousled 'do and apply makeup. She put on her red wrap dress; smiling as she thought about the first time she'd tried to wear it for Jared. Finally she was ready to go.

Emily drove her to VanBuren's, the place where Jared would be with his family. She took a couple deep, cleansing breaths and put her hand on the car door, although she didn't open the door. Emily was encouraging.

"You can do this. He told you that he would let you make up your own mind about this and you did. So go on in the door and start your new life, sweetie." She leaned over and kissed her on the cheek. "It'll be fine, Lexie, you'll see."

Alexis held on to that thought as she entered the restaurant. It was beautiful inside, but the details went right by her at the moment. She had one mission and that was to find Jared. The hostess was a very attractive young woman who was also very polite. When Alexis asked for Jared she smiled brightly and said that she would have her taken to him. She picked up the house phone and punched in some numbers while Alexis tried to look more composed than she felt. A gorgeous black woman not much taller than she was approached her with both her hands out in welcome. To Alexis's shock, she hugged her.

"Hello, Alexis. I'm Tamara, come on with me," she said happily, taking her hand and leading her through the restaurant until they came to a set of double doors marked Closed for Private Party.

To her relief, Jared was there and he walked to her with a beautiful smile on his lips. "There you are, beauty. You have no idea how happy you've made me," he said before kissing her.

"Jared, there's plenty of time for that," Tamara fussed. "You're holding things up. Let her in for the love of God."

They entered the big private dining room, for that's what it was, and Alexis readied herself for whatever reactions were to come. Jared led her to the head table and with pride in his voice, introduced her to his father and mother.

"Mom and Dad, this is the love of my life, Alexis Sharp. Alexis, meet my father, David VanBuren, and my mother."

Before he could say her name, Alexis found her voice and it was filled with wonder when she whispered, "Mrs. Lomax?"

"Oh, honey, Vanessa Lomax is the name I'm known by professionally. When I'm at home I'm Vanessa VanBuren." She came around the table to give Alexis a huge hug and whisper in her ear, "I told you that you'd be perfect for my son."

Before she could respond, his father had also claimed a hug, welcoming her to the family. "My son has excellent taste. He told us you were beautiful and he was certainly right." She could see where Jared got his good looks; the elder VanBuren was also tall, blond and devastatingly handsome. He even smiled like Jared.

The next few minutes were like being pulled into a rosy cloud of loving acceptance as she met every member of his family. Tamara was his oldest sister from Vanessa's first marriage, just as Jared was the product of his father's first marriage. She met his younger twin brothers who had the golden skin that showed them to be biracial. Lucas was the more talkative of the two. His curly golden-brown hair spiraled out in wild curls to his shoulders and his eyes twinkled.

"Damn, if I'd known they had beauties like you in Columbia, I would have been there weeks ago," he teased.

Damon was the mirror image of his twin except for his hair which was much shorter, and he, too, embraced her and welcomed her to the family. He had two children of his own, another set of twins, a boy and a girl. They looked to be about four and they were adorable, but he didn't seem to have a wife.

Jared's youngest sister, Camilla, was tall and tawny with long, thick, curly hair the color of her brothers and she, too, gave her a warm greeting. "So this is why Jared didn't want to come home. He made a new home with you. Welcome to the family, Alexis."

The introductions included Jared's grandmother. He took her over to the elderly woman's table and it became clear that she was Vanessa's mother and not Dr. VanBuren's. She was tiny but not frail; in fact she was full of vitality. "You are just as lovely as Jared said, dear. And if it makes you feel any better, I married my husband after knowing him for three weeks," she said mischievously. "My ring looks very nice on your hand," she added.

Alexis leaned down and kissed her soft brown cheek. "Thank you so much for giving it to him. It means so much to me, I can't tell you."

"Just remember that it's a gift and not a loan. You keep it on your finger, you hear?"

"It's never coming off, ever," Alexis promised.

It was much later, when she and Jared were alone at his house, that Alexis got the answers to her many questions, the main one being, "Why didn't you tell me?"

She was curled up in his lap in a big armchair near the fireplace in the master bedroom. He was holding her tight with an expression of complete contentment.

"Tell you what? That my parents were college sweethearts who got separated and met again on a vacation and they each had a child from a previous marriage? That my mother died when I was too young to remember her and that Vanessa is the only mother I've ever known? That I fell in love with her when I was three and Tamara was one-and-a-half and I've never wanted or needed anyone else because she's the sweetest person in the whole world? Is that what I didn't tell you?"

She rubbed her face against his soft, thick hair. "You know what I mean."

"Yes, I do. I didn't tell you that my mother is black for two reasons. I never tell anybody because it's not the sum total of who she is—it's simply part of her. She's so much more than her ethnicity, just like you are and I hope like I am. I deal in whole people. My brothers and sisters are just that, I don't do steps and halfs. How can someone be a half anything? And the other reason is that I needed to know that you loved me and felt safe with me for *me,* not just because my mother is black.

"I didn't want this to be one of those things where you felt comfortable with me because my family is multiracial. Either you loved me enough to be with me just for me, or you didn't."

There wasn't a lot more talking for a while, until Alexis finally murmured that she'd done his mother's hair at her spa.

"You did? She never said a word after I told her about you. I didn't even know she'd been in Columbia or on Hilton Head. She travels a lot with her work. My mom is a world-famous person. She's a sociologist, a professor, a lecturer and a writer. What a sneaky woman." He laughed. "She probably figured that I'd think she'd set us up or something."

"Emily never told me, either," Alexis remarked.

"She can't tell you what she doesn't know. Emily's never met my mother, to my knowledge. She may have met my dad, because he works at the same hospital as Todd, but she hasn't met my mother."

He kissed her again with love and passion. "Why are we wasting time talking about other people? You came to me, Alexis. You trusted me and you came to me not knowing what you were going to walk into. I love you even more now," he told her.

"So, what's next, Jared?"

"We get married, of course. We have lots of babies, lots of puppies, we travel, we love each other forever and that's about it."

"But where are we going to live? Are we staying in Chicago or what? And when are we getting married?"

He smiled at her the way he would for the rest of their lives and kissed her quiet. "Alexis, we'll work it all out together. I'm not going to try to plan everything myself and spring it one you, trust. Don't worry about it right now. Right now we have something else much more important to do."

And he took her to his bed and showed her just what she meant to him and she showed him right back.

Chapter 23

Alexis couldn't remember a better Thanksgiving. Even Aretha was elated over the news about her engagement to Jared. When Alexis called her to explain that she'd gone to Chicago to be with Jared and why she'd gone, her mother didn't try any of her usual passive-aggressive tricks, she just screamed with joy. She asked to speak to Jared and Alexis passed him the phone with a smile. They talked for a rather long time and he was smiling when they finally ended the call.

"Now do you believe me? I told you that this was meant to be, beauty. We're fated to be together and that's all there is to it."

His mother also seemed to believe that theirs was a match made in the heavens. Jared took her to his parents' house for breakfast the next day and she and Vanessa had a long talk while Jared cooked for everyone.

"Alexis, I'm so happy that you and Jared found each other," the older woman confided. "Lucie had spoken so highly of you and, when I met you, I felt an instant connection. You're just the kind of woman I've always wanted for D.J. You're smart, independent, self-reliant and you have such nice manners! If you hadn't told me that you were involved with someone, I probably would have kidnapped you and left you gift wrapped on his doorstep, that's how sure I was that you two would be perfect for one another. And you're going to give me some pretty grandbabies, too," she added mischievously. "I'm not pushing or anything, I'm just stating a fact."

Alexis was sitting on a big comfortable chair in the sunroom off the living room of the VanBuren's big house with two happy dogs in her lap. She'd been both thrilled and amused to find out that his parents had Welsh Corgis, too; a lovely male and female named Caesar and Gypsy. She was touched to her heart when Jared told her that he'd called their breeder to arrange for her to get her birthday puppies. While she was playing with the dogs, Vanessa relaxed on her chaise longue and told her how she'd met Jared's father.

"We met in college and it really was love at first sight. He was so handsome and intelligent and sweet, he just swept me off my feet! We were together for two years until my roommate, who was supposed to be my best friend, broke us up through some very calculated manipulations. She schemed and lied to him and to me while we were apart for the summer and sad to say, her plot worked beautifully for her.

"She was in love with him and she was determined to have him. It worked for a while," she said ruefully. "They got married and I was so heartbroken that I married a man I met at Martha's Vineyard the next year. David and I just started new lives without each other."

Alexis's eyes were wide and teary when she heard this, but she was too intrigued to say anything as Vanessa continued her story.

"They had Jared and then Marcy realized that she didn't want David and she didn't want to be a mother. She was more concerned with taking him away from me than with keeping him, as crazy as that sounds. She left him and the baby to be with another man. He was a pilot and they died together when his plane crashed into a mountain. David was stunned by the whole thing and he was kind of sleepwalking through life, trying to finish his residency and raise a two-year-old by himself.

"In the meantime, I really had found love with Lawrence, Tamara's father. It wasn't the wild, sweet passion I'd had with David, but it was enough. Besides, I had my baby, who was the love of my life. Sadly enough, Lawrence had a heart condition and he died of a massive heart attack, so I was a widow with a baby to raise while trying to finish my PhD. Ironically, David and I ended up vacationing at the same place, Hilton Head. We were on the beach one day, Tammie and I, and I saw a little blond boy who appeared to be lost. I went to him and he just held up his arms to me and I picked him up." She smiled fondly at the memory.

"We went back to the hotel where we were staying and there was David in the lobby with the security people and the police. He'd gone out of his mind when D.J. had wandered off so when I showed up at the hotel with Tammie on my hip and Jared by the hand he was beyond relieved. The electricity was still there and we spent the rest of our vacation together and came home as man and wife. We were fated to be together and we've loved every minute of it."

Alexis was now crying, wiping away the tears and laughing as Gypsy and Caesar tried to aid her in the process with swipes of their wet tongues.

"I'm so happy you're going to be part of our family, Alexis, and I can't wait to meet yours," Vanessa said warmly. "You and my son have some very happy years to look forward to."

Jared informed them that breakfast was ready and they went to wash their hands before entering the dining room.

Jared's father and brothers had set the table and everything looked wonderful. Like any good Southern woman, Alexis had managed to bring a hostess gift even in her haste. She had brought four jars of her homemade jams, prettily presented in glass jars with handmade labels and a ribbon around the top. When Jared's grandmother tasted the fig preserves she was in heaven.

"I haven't tasted anything like this is twenty years, Alexis. These are even better than my mother's and she was an excellent cook." She looked at Jared and smiled her approval. "You did us proud, Jared. You're going to have a very happy life with your Alexis. I'm so happy for you two."

Jared was seated next to Alexis and he leaned over and kissed her with a great deal of love. "Thank you, Grams. The only thing that could make me any happier was if we were married right now."

When the VanBuren family converged on Columbia after the holiday, the same sentiment was expressed often, at least by Jared and Alexis. They wanted to get married immediately with no fuss and no fanfare, an idea that was vetoed by everyone else. Both families had a chance to express their collective opinions during the first week of December. The notion of a small intimate wedding was voted down by everyone. Alexis's family and Jared's were in one accord on this one; there was going to be a big glorious wedding to join the two of them in holy matrimony.

Alexis was delighted that her beloved aunt BeBe came down from New York to meet Jared and his family. Aunt BeBe was her mother's younger sister and she was a well-known stage actress in New York. "Sweetie, you did good," she praised Alexis when she saw her with Jared. The families were at Seven-Seventeen for the soft opening night combined with an engagement party.

A soft opening meant that the restaurant would open for business without advertising, which gave the staff a chance to work out all the kinks before the grand opening. Once the grand opening was announced, there would be press coverage and an extensive ad campaign during which time everything from decor to service to food had to be perfect. Everything was pretty much perfect now, as far as Alexis could see. She toured the restaurant with Jared and marveled at how beautiful the end product was. Sydney was right there with the two of them, eager to see everything, especially the kitchen. Jared picked her up and carried her into the busy place, staying well out of the way of Lucas, who was acting as chef, and all the line cooks. Sydney was most impressed with the operation, especially with Lucas, who flirted with her madly.

"He's your brother right, Uncle Jared? So when you marry my aunt Alexis, he'll be my uncle, too?"

Lucas overheard her and winked one of his pretty eyes at her. "I'll be anything you want me to be, sweetie. I can be your uncle Lucas if you want."

She giggled her agreement and looked positively bashful, an unusual state for her.

After a long evening of champagne toasts, great food and lots of laughter, Jared and Alexis headed for her house and some much-desired privacy. As he drove, he looked at her with his heart in his eyes and said, "I don't think can we elope at this point, beauty."

She leaned against the headrest and agreed. "Not if we want to live. How about Valentine's Day?"

"Swell. I can wait that long but not a day longer."

"I agree. I talked to my sister Adrienne and she'll be home by Christmas. I wish she was here now because she's in favor of quick and fast, too."

Jared laughed quietly. "I'm going to like Adrienne, I can just feel it."

* * *

Despite their misgivings, the wedding was wonderful. It was big and it was beautiful, according to everyone who attended. Alexis wore an astounding strapless white gown with lavish red embroidery on the bodice, and all around the skirt, including an overlay that led down into the train. She carried a round bouquet of deep red roses and calla lilies and her eyes sparkled like the diamonds in her ears. Her attendants were Sherri as maid of honor, Emily as matron of honor and Alana, Adrienne, Ava, Tamara and Camilla as her bridesmaids. They all wore fabulous red strapless dresses with high slits on the side. Sydney and Damon's daughter, Courtney, were flower girls and his son, Gabriel, was the ring bearer. Jared's brothers were the best men, and the groomsmen were Roland, Todd, Javier and two more of Jared's closest friends from Chicago. The wedding was held at Hightower AME and the reception was at Seven-Seventeen.

It was a huge party, with the best food anyone had ever had, all prepared by Jared's team. Besides the luscious cocktail buffet of Kobe Beef skewers and miniature Saucisse Minuit and bacon-wrapped shrimp, there was a sit-down dinner of beef short ribs, grilled salmon and roast chicken with amazing side dishes. A dessert buffet with all kinds of Southern specialties like pecan tarts, red velvet cupcakes, mini pound cakes and individual peach cobblers flanked the five-tier almond cake with passion fruit filling and white chocolate frosting. When the guests were eating, they were dancing to a special surprise; Jared's father had flown the jazz quintet that he and his friends had played in for years and they jammed the night away.

Alexis and Jared had a special dance that they performed as another surprise. They started out with a romantic slow dance to Donny Hathaway's "You Were Meant for Me" and segued into Beyoncé's "Love on Top" which had everyone laughing and applauding as they executed expert steps to the lively music. At the song's end, everyone was taking the dance floor except Adrienne, who was looking a little green around the gills.

Alana went with her to the ladies' room where she promptly tossed up her dinner. Alana dampened paper towels and patted her sister's face, asking her if she had the flu or something.

Adrienne's face, so like her sisters with its velvety skin and dainty features, twisted into a wry expression. "That would be 'or something.' I'm pretty sure I'm pregnant, Alana. It's a good thing the wedding was this week because, if I'm right, next week I wouldn't have fit into this gown," she added.

Alana couldn't think of a single thing to say—something that had never happened to her in her life.

Meanwhile the party went on and it was time for Alexis to throw her bouquet. Even though her back was turned and several women were reaching for it, it fell right into Sherri's hands. Lucas caught the garter and gave her a rakish grin.

"Looks like we're the next ones to get married, Sherri," he said in his sexy voice.

Sydney smiled brightly and said, "Then you're better than an uncle Lucas, you get to be my daddy!"

Sherri laughed merrily, but she missed the glint in Lucas's eyes. Jared didn't, though. He smiled down at his bride and whispered, "Sherri better get some good running shoes because I recognize that look. If she doesn't intend to be my new sister-in-law very soon, she'd better get a head start on him."

Knowing what she did about the VanBuren men, Alexis agreed wholeheartedly before giving her husband one more kiss.

* * * * *

*Some things
are worth
waiting for…*

ANY WAY
YOU
WANT IT

MAUREEN
SMITH

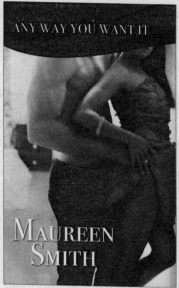

Zandra Kennedy owes the success of her elite escort agency
to some simple rules. Her girls offer companionship, not sex.
And business always comes first. Sandra won't allow any man
to rule her life the way her father dominated her mother.
But when a Caribbean vacation with her childhood friend,
gorgeous former navy SEAL Remington Brand, leads to an
erotic encounter, she realizes she's not immune to true passion.

Only, Remy is hiding a secret…a betrayal that could shatter
Zandra's career…and their newfound future.

**"This is a spicy boy-meets-girl tale that will keep you turning
the pages. Make sure you wear flameproof gloves!"**
—*RT Book Reviews* on *WHATEVER YOU LIKE*

HARLEQUIN®
www.Harlequin.com

*Available December 2012
wherever books are sold!*

REQUEST YOUR FREE BOOKS!

2 FREE NOVELS
PLUS 2 FREE GIFTS!

KIMANI™
ROMANCE

Love's ultimate destination!

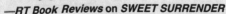